ROCKETPACK ADVENTURES

RUSS CROSSLEY   LESLEY L. SMITH   RITA SCHULZ

KELLY CAIRO   BARBARA G. TARN   R. G. HART

MARY JO RABE   DEANNA KNIPPLING   JAMIE FERGUSON

CHUCK ANDERSON   JIM LEMAY

53RD STREET PUBLISHING

TABLE OF CONTENTS

INTRODUCTION

What you are about to read was sparked by watching of one of my favorite movie serials, 1949's King of the Rocketmen. The film is twelve black and white chapters of action and adventure as Professor Jeff King fights the evil Dr. Vulcan's plan to destroy New York City with a Sonic Decimator. Dr. King dons a rocketpack and a helmet, to hide his identity, before he flies into action against Dr. Vulcan and his minions. Rays guns, hats that never come off in fist-fights, and primitive controls for the rocket to go up or down make this a cliffhanger of a serial. There were several other serials made by Republic Pictures with characters donning flying rocket suits in the years following this film and all are great fun.

The Rocketeer revived excitement in the genre briefly in 1991 with the release of a major motion picture. And IDW comics have been issuing miniseries featuring the hero since 1982 until the last reported mention I could find in 2014. Disney has reportedly had a movie reboot in the works since 2016 so who knows we might even get another Rocketeer film some day.

Considering this history I thought it might be fun to revisit this genre once again in the anthology you see before you. Ten stories of rocket and jetpack wearing beings some in the future, some in the past, and some in alternate realities written by these talented authors taking on the genre with rockets blazing.

We all hope you enjoy these stories and hope you will seek out works by these dedicated authors who work so hard to provide you the best in modern adventure fiction.

Have fun,
    Russ Crossley
    2018

MERCENARY KNIGHTS

A Blaster Squad Short Story
Russ Crossley

Sol System
  Earth
  European Asian Confederation
  Beijing
  4146.5.15 Galactic

Nick Justice shifted in his seat, his eyes fixed on the two contestants inside the vast antigravity dome beyond the plasti-steel wall, their images enhanced on the massive view screen stretching across the wall of the arena across from the spectator seating. The knights wore blast armor and helmets to protect them from the blows they were surely about to suffer in combat.

There were at least seventy rows between Nick and the wall and a hundred above him filled with tens of thousands of eager spectators. This vast crowd moved like waves on a stormy sea, their voices an overlapping jumble of nervous energy and expectation for the impending battle between the two rocket pack-wearing knights in the arena.

The air was rife with a heady mix of smells that filled Nick's senses: cheeseburgers, fried lode fish from Parsis III, a variety of alcoholic beverages from rich Icelandic ale to the vinegary Phobos wine preferred in a few of the Martian domes. Onlookers came from all over the Alliance to see these games. This was Nick's first time.

The two knights stood on hoverboards that to Nick looked like surfboards, with their booted feet secured in stirrups built into the boards. They hovered in the air about five meters above the deck plating at opposite ends of the arena facing each other. They gripped laser lances in gloved hands and were leaning forward, ready to fire their back-mounted rocket packs once the announcer gave the signal.

Personally, Nick had never enjoyed blood sports and he was unfamiliar with this one. Rocket pack jousting had been a spectator sport for the past seven hundred and seventeen years. The difference this time, and what brought him here, was that two of his team were among those competing for the million-credit top prize. He didn't want to see them injured or killed, but he also couldn't deny them their favorite pastimes when on leave.

During shore leave on Earth, Bones and the Kid had bonded over their shared love of outrageous—and often dangerous—sports, both as spectators, and all too often for Nick's comfort, as participants. He'd been with them at the Space Race Bar and Grill when, after a night of imbibing far too much whiskey, they'd agreed to take part in the Galactic Jousting Championships. Nick had hoped they'd be disqualified since they weren't on the professional jousting circuit, but since they knew many fellow sporting enthusiasts on the inside of the organizing committee, they were soon cleared to compete.

Nick's stomach tightened as he heard the Estuian announcer's high-pitched voice yell, "Go!"

The two knights activated their rocket packs and shot forward, their plasma rockets shooting them to high speeds as they raced at each other. They wore different colored armor, one sky blue, the other crimson red, so the spectators knew which pilot was which during the impending battle.

Just before coming into contact range, the blue knight swung his hoverboard sharply to the left until he was ninety degrees to his opponent. Too late, the red knight must have realized he was in danger because he tried to swing his hoverboard sharply to the right but only managed to get partway before the blue knight deployed his laser lance to stab the red knight in his helmet. The red pilot was off balance so was unable to parry the blow. There was an explosion of sparks as the tip of the laser lance struck home, then the two boards raced past each other.

The red knight was still standing, but given the way he swayed, Nick knew he was dazed. The tip of his lance drooped as if he were struggling to hold its weight level. And the red knight's flight path appeared erratic rather than the smooth flight from before.

The blue knight swung his hoverboard around and shot after his disoriented opponent. In keeping with the rules, after a knight had struck the first blow, they didn't have to return to the starting position. They could now attack at will, and that was exactly what the blue knight was doing. In most matches it took several jousts before either contestant landed a blow. They were required to keep returning to the starting position to try again until first contact. After the first blow landed, the match was usually decided fairly quickly.

When the knights landed blows simultaneously, it occasionally resulted in total destruction of the boards, the rocket packs, and sometimes both combatants. But in most cases, only one knight successfully landed the first blow. Though rare, there had even been decapitations.

Nick held his breath as the blue knight rapidly approached the red knight from behind. His mouth dried and his heart beat faster. *Come on, red, turn around.*

Around him the crowd was shouting encouragement, some calling for the blue knight to kill the red knight. The taste of sour bile rose at the back of Nick's throat. Obviously these people and aliens had never been in a real fight like those Blaster Squad had been in many times. He'd seen enough blood and death in battle that dying during a game seemed absurd and a waste of supposedly intelligent life.

The blue knight raised his lance and leaned forward in his stirrups, obviously bracing for impact. It looked like the red knight had no chance to survive the encounter. But at the last second, the red knight's board shot vertically out of range and the blue knight's board flew under his prey, missing the target completely. The red knight flew his board in a loop until level with the blue knight and was now within range of a strike.

A quick thrust pierced the blue knight's back and he went limp, the hoverboard spinning out of control. It struck the wall before continuing on a rapid descent to the floor of the arena. The red knight steered up and away to be clear of his opponent should his board explode after the bone-shattering impact.

The blue knight slumped forward, his arms hanging limp at his sides, man and machine dropping like a stone, smoke trailing from the damaged hoverboard. They impacted the floor of the arena at high speed, the board shattering into multiple pieces in a burst of smoke and flame. The blue knight's body was tossed like a rag doll from the board before it exploded, landing on the deck a few meters away. Nick had seen enough corpses to know the red knight was definitely very dead.

The crowd around him went wild, cheering, enthusiastic applause, some people and aliens screaming the blue knight's name, which happened to be Bloody Helios Ark. Nick surmised this fellow was either some sort of local hero or was well known on the pro circuit. Either way, he was glad Bones and Gears didn't have to face this man. He was good—very good. Too good.

But his relief was short-lived. The announcer's voice erupted from the hidden comm speakers installed throughout the arena facility, silencing the crowd. "That's the conclusion of the singles matches. Once the wreckage is removed, we will be starting our team matches. First up are the Terror Twins, Nok and Prat Mukelson, two well-known Lobsan knights out to compete in their fifteenth match and hopefully twenty-second kills."

The announcer paused to let the audience cheer and stomp their feet, signaling their approval of this team of Lobsans. The four-limbed aliens were taller and bulkier than humans and fierce warriors known for their very ornery tempers. Nick's stomach knotted in fear for his friends. Surely they must have realized by now that participating in these games was a terrible idea.

No sooner had Nick reached that conclusion than two new knights appeared from the left side of the arena through an opening in the wall just as the last of the wreckage, and the broken body of the blue knight, disappeared in the sparkling energy of a materializer beam. The new contestants were covered head-to-toe in gleaming black armor and they each held over their heads a laser lance. They were thrusting their arms as if they'd already won the impending joust to wind up the crowd, which it did. Though not in the way they must have hoped.

The arena seating area erupted with the spontaneous sounds of jeers, boos, curses, and shrill whistles. So much so that Nick had to cover his ears in an attempt to block the cacophony of noise assaulting his senses and penetrating his body.

Though the helmets covered their faces, Nick recognized the form of the tall, muscular half-Martian weapons specialist, Bones, and the lean muscled form of the Kid, Blaster Squad's demolitions specialist, standing beside him. They appeared unfazed by the crowds contemptuous taunting of them pumping their arms vigorously.

Nick took a long drink from his cup of lemon water to moisten his dry throat, then dropped the empty cup to his feet.

"Hey, buddy, watch it," said a familiar voice beside him.

Shifting his gaze to his right, he discovered Siren seated beside him with a large bag of popcorn. How long had she been there? "Hiya, Captain. Have I missed anything good?"

Nick eyed his second-in-command. "The last singles match just ended."

She nodded. "Yeah, I saw that mess. The red knight kicked butt." Her long, delicate fingers dipped into the bag of hot buttered popcorn and came out with a few of the popped kernels that she tossed into her mouth. Her almond-shaped yellow eyes sparkled with delight at his confusion. Her long coal-black hair was tied into a ponytail that draped down her back. She was wearing one of her skintight one-piece suits that accentuated her lean, muscular figure. She was deadly in a straight-up fight and exceedingly loyal to the Squad. She'd saved Nick's life too many times to count.

She offered him the bag. "Want some?"

He snorted. "No. Thanks. I'm a little nervous."

Her brow wrinkled. "About what?"

"Do you even know what's happening?" Nick asked, waving his right hand toward the vast arena beyond the glass wall. "Our friends are going to die."

She laughed. "No, they're not. They're Blaster Squad."

Nick thought about it for a few seconds, then shrugged. She was right. Bones and the Kid had survived impossible odds to cheat death so many times that jousting with a rocket pack on your back didn't seem all that dangerous.

"Gentle beings," said the announcer over the arena wide comm, "our challengers for this match are Rocky Bones and Alfonso The Kid Ripe, known collectively as the Mercenary Knights. Both are experienced, decorated mercenaries fresh from the badlands where they vanquished countless enemies of the Alliance." The announcer paused to allow time for more boos and heckling, and thankfully, a smattering of applause, which eased Nick's trepidation somewhat.

"Are we ready?" asked the announcer, followed by thunderous applause and screams of ecstasy and shouts for blood. "Go!"

Nick locked his eyes on the arena. Over the crowd noise he heard the distinctive sounds of popcorn being eaten; then the smell of warm butter wafted over him. *How can she eat at a time like this*?

In the arena he watched Bones and the Kid fire their rocket packs and shoot toward the two Lobsans, who made no move at all toward their opponents. What were the alien warriors doing?

As they flew, Bones and the Kid started to separate, Bones going high and the Kid flying low. It was a classic flanking maneuver designed to simulate being surrounded and hopefully preventing a coordinated dual counterattack. It would be every being for themselves.

Nick swallowed hard and beads of perspiration began to trail down his back. He mentally crossed all of his fingers and toes, not that he believed in luck.

The Kid stabbed at the Lobsan on the right, who deflected the blow with the shaft of his lance. The Kid then reversed his rocket and sped out of range of the alien's lance as he launched a counterattack. This was going to take longer than the previous match.

Bones distracted the other alien knight by suddenly dipping under the alien's defensive thrust and striking the Lobsan's hoverboard with his lance. The Lobsan's board seemed unaffected but it might be moving slower, at least to Nick's unpracticed eye.

These two Lobsans were experienced knights who obviously had won many jousts. They could be playing possum, waiting to see how the two rookie knights would attack before deciding on a winning strategy. At least that's how Nick would have done it.

Bones and the Kid flew to a point about ten meters above the two alien knights and stopped, hovering in place for several seconds. They turned their backs to each other, extended their laser lances in front of them, then began to loop down and around their foes intending to strike the two Lobsan knights in a series of repetitive strikes.

The Lobsans must have anticipated the attack because they split up and shot toward Bones' and the Kid's flight paths. They struck simultaneously at Bones' and the Kid's hoverboards, disabling them.

The badly damaged boards fell out of the air as they spiraled out of control. Tossing off their lances, Bones and the Kid separated from their hoverboards before the boards smashed into the deck and exploded. Bones and the Kid hovered over the deck using their rocket packs' adjustable twinjets to make elaborate moves back and forth, reminiscent of caged animals. They appeared unharmed but were now unarmed as they waited for the two Lobsan knights' follow-up attack.

The aliens didn't hesitate. Diving toward the unarmed Bones and the Kid, their rocket packs' thrusters on full power, the tremendous roar of the jet wash made the glass wall rattle sending a renewed wave of excitement through the crowd of onlookers. The two Lobsans flew at the mercenaries. The Lobsans' lances were held at the ready, preparing to strike death blows. Nick held his breath, his heart beating hard. How would his friends survive with no weapons to defend themselves?

The two Lobsan knights spiraled downward, growing ever closer to Nick's defenseless friends. Nick wanted to break through the glass wall and help them.

"Don't even think about it," cautioned Siren. Her breath smelled of buttered popcorn. "They frown on spectators interfering in a legal joust around here." He glanced at her. "And by *frowning,* I mean they shoot anyone who interrupts a fight." She smirked, then continued to stuff popcorn in her mouth.

He turned his attention back to his friends, hovering over the deck, and saw that the two alien knights were almost on top of them. Suddenly Bones and the Kid pulled out laser swords and parried the thrusts of the incoming lances at the last second. The two aliens were thrown off balance by the mercenaries' attack and their hoverboards went out of control due to the sudden weight imbalance.

To Nick's shock, the hoverboards contacted Bones and the Kid and all four beings became tangled together, quickly slamming to the deck with a loud bang and erupting in a massive, fiery explosion. Thick black smoke billowed from the crash site, obscuring the spectators' view of the four combatants. Nick rose to his feet, as did much of the vast crowd surrounding him. Siren was the exception, preferring to stay seated and continue to enjoy her snack as if nothing serious was happening.

Doesn't she care about Bones and the Kid? wondered Nick.

"Gentle beings," interrupted the announcer, his voice calm and authoritative, "please stay in your seats while our emergency technicians attend the crash site."

Two shimmering figures solidified next to the billowing wall of fire and smoke. They were humanoid, but whether they were aliens or humans, Nick was unable to tell since they wore head-to-toe emergency suits that hid their faces and other identifying features. The suits protected the technicians from fire, smoke, possible secondary explosions, and they provided independent breathing, heating, and cooling systems to allow the technician to get to any accident victims without risk to themselves.

The two technicians disappeared into the fire and smoke. The stadium comm came to life, allowing the audience to hear communications between the technicians and the announcer. "What do you see?" asked the announcer.

"We're almost there," said a distinctive female voice. Her voice was calm with an edge of huskiness. Breathing sounds followed until there was a grunt. "We found the crash," said a high-pitched male voice.

"Are they alive?" asked the announcer.

There was a pause that seemed an eternity to Nick until finally the female technician said, "Unknown. Their bodies are not among the wreckage."

Nick looked open-mouthed at Siren, who grinned at him from her seat. "Wanna go?" she said cheerily.

"Where are we going?"

She stood and dropped the now empty popcorn bag on her seat. "You'll see," she said cryptically, a sly smile on her lips.

He followed her, making their way past the shocked audience members. Along the way he heard a variety of explanations in an attempt to understand what they had collectively just watched. Some speculated that the four knights had been vaporized in the explosion, or that they had used personal materializer transport devices to disappear, or that a trap door opened underneath them at the moment of the crash and closed after they'd escaped.

From experience in many combat missions, Nick didn't think any of these options were reasonable, other than perhaps the materializer transport. But such an escape would have to be perfectly timed or they'd be transporting corpses. An explosion such as this one created a shock wave of such force the victim had very little chance of surviving. Shock often stopped the heart or impaired breathing from the sudden increase in pressure on the chest.

Siren reached the lifts and Nick ran to catch up just as the twin doors slid open. Siren stepped in and Nick joined her before the doors closed. No one else had followed them. "Siren, what's going on? I want to see what happened to Bones and the Kid."

Siren looked at him knowingly. "That's exactly where we're going."

Nick was tiring of these games. "Siren, you're my second-in-command. I order you to cut out this cryptic crap and be straight me with."

Siren feigned surprise, arching her thin eyebrows. "I *am* being *straight*. Captain."

Nick sighed and avoided her by looking at the floor of the lift car. "I'm sorry, Siren. I'm upset about the loss of Bones and the Kid." His voice caught. Choking back a sob, he cleared his throat. "They were not only great team members but good friends—"

Siren covered her mouth with one hand to stifle a laugh. Before Nick could respond to this sudden burst of inappropriate humor, the lift doors opened.

Two very tall, muscular Alliance Navy troopers dressed in gray and blue fatigues stood beyond the lift doors, their gray faces stern, their humorless eyes scanning the interior of the lift car. "Captain Justice?" asked the trooper on Nick's right, his voice gruff.

"Yes, and this is my second-in-command, Commander Sirenna Albright."

"Would you and Commander Albright accompany us to the waiting area, sir?"

Nick studied the faces of the two navy troopers. There was no hint of aggression or deception on their rugged, square-jawed features or in their dark eyes. "Lead the way."

The troopers turned around and started toward the gray tiled hallway in front of them. The hallway walls were unadorned and painted a simple white. The sounds of their boots echoed in the silence as they walked. It felt vaguely unsettling with the absence of the crowd noises in the crowded arena.

Crimson red signs painted on the walls at various points were directing them to a waiting area designated for combatants. Nick wondered why they were going there.

Finally they arrived at a set of glass doors with the words "Combatant Waiting Room" painted on the frosted glass. The guard who spoke earlier turned toward them. "We will wait outside, sir. Please enter."

The troopers took up positions on either side of the doors and stood at ease, their hands behind their backs. It was then Nick noticed they wore blaster pistols, which was unusual when on leave on Earth. This meant these two were on duty at a sporting event. Why? The doors opened, providing an unexpected answer.

"Nick! How good to see you." Behind the greeting was the smiling face of Edgar Whizzar, Chair of the Alliance Council. No wonder there were armed navy personnel here. The Chair has been under threat since the attacks on Alliance planets began more than two years ago. The doors closed behind them.

"Edgar? What's happenin—" His words caught in his throat when a smiling Bones and Kid appeared from behind the Chair. Their battle armor was blackened and they seemed a little singed around the edges, but they were otherwise unharmed.

"Bones! Kid!" He ran to them and clapped them both on the shoulder. "I thought for sure you'd been killed. Siren didn't, but I did." Nick stopped and cast an annoyed glance at his second-in-command. "You knew they weren't hurt all along, didn't you?"

She nodded, her lips forming a wide grin.

The Kid laughed. "The Chair arranged with the organizing committee for this jousting tournament to transport us out at the moment of impact."

Nick's eyes must have revealed his next question because Bones added, "Don't be concerned about the two Lobsan knights. They were transported out as well. Everyone is safe and unharmed." Nick reminded himself why he didn't play poker with these guys.

Of course he had never played poker, but his grandfather once told him most people had *shows* that revealed what they were thinking. It was part of the game, explained his grandfather. Nick had no idea what exactly a *show* entailed but his grandfather was usually correct about such things. Evidently Bones had easily read his *show*.

Nick scanned the smiling faces of his friends and the Chair. "You mean this is all fake?"

"Yes, Nick," said Siren with a chuckle. "It's called show business."

Nick considered her words. "Ya know, I kind of like the idea of mercenary knights."

This elicited a chorus of laughter. Nick joined in as the relief of knowing his friends were safe washed over him.

ABOUT THE AUTHOR

International selling Star Trek author, Russ Crossley, writes science fiction and fantasy, and mystery/suspense as well as their various subgenres. His latest science fiction short novels involve the mercenary team, Blaster Squad. Set in the far future this fast paced, action adventure series is available in print, ebook, and now books 1, 2, and 3 are available as audio books. The 7th and final book in the current story line will be available soon.

He has sold several short stories that have appeared in anthologies from various publishers including; WMG Publishing, Pocket Books, 53rd Street Publishing, and St. Martins Press. He is past president of the Greater Vancouver Chapter of Romance Writers of America. He is also an alumni of the Oregon Coast Professional Fiction Writers Master Class taught by award winning author/editors, Kristine Katherine Rusch and Dean Wesley Smith.

Feel free to contact him on Facebook, Twitter, or his website http//:www.russcrossley.com. He loves to hear from readers.

GIRL POWER

Girl Power

Lesley L. Smith

"Brittani!" my grandmother yelled, in a totally dignified manner, of course. She said a lady is always dignified.

I jerked in surprise and dropped the canister of hydrogen peroxide. It clanged loudly when it hit the concrete floor. I was in Mom's workshop in our converted garage. It was full of workbenches and shelves of her equipment and inventions. Mom herself was no longer with us. But being in her workshop made me feel close to her.

Grandmother appeared in the doorway. "What was that noise? What are you doing in here, young lady?" Without letting me answer her, she plowed ahead. "If I've told you once, I've told you a thousand times, this workshop is dangerous." She sighed and frowned. "Come on. You're going to be late for school."

I knew she missed Mom as much as I did. It's why she hadn't gotten rid of Mom's stuff. And I couldn't fault her for trying to take care of me. I was all she had left. Five years ago my parents both died in a steam car accident. (I still avoided anything steam-powered if I could help it.)

I walked to Grandmother and gave her a hug.

She actually let me hug her for a few seconds. Then, she sniffed and said, "That's enough of that. Hurry now or you're going to miss your zeppelin." That would be bad. That would definitely make me late, and I couldn't afford any more tardies.

She pointed back towards my bedroom. "And don't forget your Girl Guide uniform. You have a meeting after school."

"Yes, ma'am." But I would never forget Girl Guides. Our local chapter of Girl Guides were all my BFFs. They'd helped me get through some really tough times. They were my sisters.

Very unfortunately, the rumor-mill said the national organization was struggling. I'd find out the truth today at the meeting.

The 5-minute warning went off on my beautiful new fon. It had a metal case with a round metal-edged screen and a metal rotary dial (with a shiny brass finish). "Oh no!" I shoved my fon in my pocket, ran to my room, grabbed my already-packed backpack, ran down the hall and out the front door.

I sprinted for the zeppelin stop. It was a beautiful fall day, and the yellow, orange and red leaves were like stained glass hanging on the trees. It was warm enough for my light-weight school uniform, so good choice there.

Down at the end of the block, the zeppelin was already descending to the stop. Oh no. I put on speed.

I reached the stop just as the last person was ascending the gangplank. It was one of my best friends, Emma. I hurried after her, jumping on to the gangplank and striding up to the landing, a small wooden balcony hanging off the zeppelin.

Just as I stepped through the doorway into the dis/embarkation lounge, the porter yelled, "All aboard." They retracted the gangplank.

"Hi, Emma," I said, grinning and panting a little, glad I'd made it.

"Hi, Brittani." She grinned back. "You should really consider going out for track."

"Wait! Wait!" a male voice called out from below. We glanced down through the still-open doorway. It was a boy from our school. He held out his gangly arm like he was going to grab the now-retracted gangplank. Yeah, good luck with that.

Emma smirked. "Too bad, so sad. He's going to get a tardy." The zeppelins had very strict schedules. If you missed your stop, you were pretty screwed. They were quite restricted in where and when they could fly because of winds near the ground and other factors.

The engines revved and we started moving off towards school.

"Why were you almost late again?" she asked.

"I was checking out Mom's rocket-pack again, more specifically the fuel. When she was alive, you couldn't get the concentrated pure hydrogen peroxide you needed. But I just got some new stuff."

"Really?" She raised her eyebrows. "You bought rocket fuel? That sounds dangerous. Is it dangerous?"

"Nah." I shook my head. "Hydrogen peroxide is stable as long it doesn't come in contact with a catalyst. And the beauty of Mom's jet-pack was she designed a way to increase the exhaust velocity. If she hadn't died, she would have made a ton of money. Everybody would be riding around in jet-packs instead of zeppelins and those dangerous steam cars. She was an inventor, you know."

"I know," Emma said quietly, and put her hand on my arm.

At her sympathy, I had to blink back tears.

"I know you still miss her," she said. "And your dad."

I couldn't talk for a moment. I cleared my throat. "So, Girl Guides, after school. Are you going?"

"Of course!" she said. "Wouldn't miss it!"

After school, me and the rest of the Girl Guides met in the Spanish room, surrounded by giant Hola's, Amigo's and Buenos Días's cut out of colored construction paper and stuck on the wall.

All day, my brain had been percolating. What if the rumors were true? What if Girl Guides were in trouble? It would break my heart if I lost my Girl Guide sisters.

How could we save them?

Señora Gonzalez pounded the gavel on her desk. "Hear ye, hear ye, I bring this meeting of the Girl Guides to order."

Emma whispered, "Is it just me or does she overdo the parliamentary procedure?"

"It's not just you," I whispered back. "But Grandmother says it's tradition." Grandmother had been a Girl Guide when she was younger. She said Girl Guides had taught her how to be a lady. And Mom was a Girl Guide too. I loved following in their footsteps.

Señora Gonzalez glared at me. I shut up and gave her my attention.

"We commence with the reading of the minutes from the last meeting," she said.

My mind wandered again. I was dying to try out Mom's rocketpack with the new fuel. How long would the rocket last? How far could I go?

I glanced around the room. And I was dying to save this group. We helped people, did good deeds and I'd made a lot of good friends, best friends, sisters, even. It was well worth saving. I knew I didn't have the power to save my parents, but maybe I had the power to save Girl Guides.

I had to save it.

"All in favor of ratifying the minutes?" Señora Gonzalez said.

We all held up our hands and said, "Aye."

"So, that brings us to new business," she said, slowly, and frowned. She was silent for moment.

"Something's up," Emma whispered.

"Definitely," I whispered back.

The room filled with anticipation as the silence grew.

Finally, Señora Gonzalez said, "As you may have heard, the group is in danger of losing funding. The national chapter is calling on all Girl Guides to put on their thinking caps to try to think of ways to raise money. Use your imagination! Be creative!"

We all looked at each other. It was hard to be creative when ordered to be creative.

Emma raised her hand and said, "What if we can't think of anything right this minute?"

Señora Gonzalez smiled. "I didn't mean for you to think of something right now. Let it percolate. And that brings us to something that has already percolated: the fall gig and festival..."

Señora Gonzalez' advice to let our ideas percolate must have gone straight to the creative parts of my brain because as soon as the meeting let out I had an idea.

"Hey, guys," I said to my cohort Emma, Olivia, and Ava (we four usually shared a tent on our camping trips), "I have an idea." We were all packing up our stuff.

"I knew it!" Emma said. "I knew you'd think of something." She always had my back.

"What is it?" Olivia asked. She put her unzipped pack on her back and a notebook fell out. She leaned down to get it. She was the free-spirit of the group, and, yes, a little disorganized.

"Yeah," Ava said. "Spill." She was already totally ready to go. Her stuff was always squared away. She said that's how engineers were.

"I think..." I said.

My three BFFs stepped closer, with bated breath.

"I think I can get Mom's rocket-pack to work--with your help," I said.

"That sounds fun." Emma smiled. "As long as you're sure it's not dangerous."

"It's safe," I said.

"But how does this help Girl Guides?" Ava asked.

Olivia was putting her backpack on again.

"If, er, I mean, when, we get them to work we can sell them and use the money for Girl Guides," I said.

"Awesome!" There were awesomes all around. That's what I'm talking about.

❀

Back at Mom's workshop, the four of us had put down our stuff and rolled up our sleeves.

"So this is Mom's rocket-pack," I said, holding up a metal framework that resembled that of a regular backpack---but with a metal plate along the back.

"Neat," Olivia said. "But it looks complicated."

"That's it?" Ava took a step closer. "It sort of looks like a backpack." She fingered it. "Nice design. Nice welding."

I nodded. "Mom was good."

"Yeah," Emma said, "and look, the fuel canisters click in there." She pointed at the rounded metal struts.

"Exactly." I grinned at them. I knew bringing them in to help was the right thing to do.

"What do you want us to do?" Ava asked.

"Can I test it out?" Olivia asked bouncing up and down. "Can I? It looks really fun!"

I didn't want anyone to get hurt. I didn't think they would, but better safe than sorry. "You better let me do it," I said. "It might be dangerous."

Emma shot me a sharp look. "You said it wasn't dangerous."

"Just in case," I said.

"Well, I'll get the first aid kit ready--just in case," Emma said.

"This is fun!" Olivia said.

I carefully hooked up the canisters of new propellant to the rocket-pack and then strapped it on my back. It was heavy. It felt like I had all the books of my entire scholarly career on my back at the same time.

"One of you record what happens with your fon," I said, taking a slow step towards the door. "One of you time how long I stay in the air." We all walked into the back yard.

"Aren't you worried at all about wearing a rocket on your back?" Olivia asked.

"Of course not," I said. "Mom knew what she was doing." I believed in her one hunderd percent.

"How strong an exothermic reaction are we talking about?" Ava asked.

"These exhaust gases are cooler than other propellants," I said. "Come on." I opened the door to the backyard and stepped out.

They followed, Ava frowning a little, Emma frowning a lot, and Olivia bouncing.

"Are you sure about this?" Emma asked.

"Yes," I said. "Get ready"

They held up their fons.

"I'll count down from three," Emma said.

I nodded, pulse racing. This was so exciting! Me and my friends were powerful. We could make things happen. I felt like Mom was with us, watching, helping and cheering us on.

"Three, two, one, blast off!" Emma said.

They all pointed their fons at me.

I activated the rockets.

Immediately, I sort of jumped up about three feet, jerking left and right. The fuel sort of spit out unevenly.

Then, my feet started feeling very warm. Hot. I smelled smoke. Uh oh.

"Turn it off!" Emma said.

I turned it off and landed back on my feet on the ground with a jar. I looked down. My shoes and socks looked black. But nothing hurt, thank goodness.

I was disappointed. How could Mom's awesome invention not

work? I'd checked over everything and it seemed good. Her design was solid and the pack totally matched the design.

Emma was already rushing towards me with the first aid kit. "Are you all right? Did you get burned?" She led me to a stool in the workshop.

"I was watching the exhaust." Ava took the jet-pack from me. "I think something's wrong with the emitters."

"Yeah," Olivia said. "It's like that time when my fancy perfume got clogged and just dribbled out instead of spraying evenly. I had to clean the little dispenser-thingy at the top."

I grinned. Leave it to Olivia to compare a rocket to perfume.

"I think she's right," Ava said. "Do you have some solvent to clean them?"

They were both right. The design was solid, like I thought. It was just old and had gotten dirty some how. "Yeah." I pointed at the solvent on the shelf. "But be careful..."

"It's hot, I know," Ava said.

Ava and Olivia carefully cleaned the emitters while Emma took off my shoes and socks.

"Seriously, Em?" I asked. "I can take off my own shoes and socks. And besides, there's nothing wrong with my feet. I would feel it if they were burned."

"I'm just checking." She held up one of my feet, staring at it.

I wiggled my toes at her.

She grinned. "Yeah, looks okay."

Ava and Olivia finished cleaning the emitters. I put my socks and shoes back on.

"Are you sure you want to try it again?" Emma asked.

I buckled the rocket-pack back on and stood staring at my friends. "Yes. I believe in Mom and her invention. And I believe in us. We can do this together. We have the power, together."

"Okay," Emma said. "I trust you."

"I'm excited!" Olivia said, bouncing up and down.

"Me, too," Ava said in a quiet voice. "I have a good feeling about this."

The four of us traipsed into the back yard.

Emma counted down. "Three, two, one, blast off!"

I turned it on and shot ten feet straight up into the air, and then kept going a little more slowly.

They were all pointing their fons at me.

"All right, Brittani!" they yelled. "You rock!"

"Hey, look out for the zeppelin!" Ava yelled.

"Yeah!" Olivia yelled.

"Be careful," Emma yelled.

I looked up and realized I was fast approaching a zeppelin. I swerved, stepped onto the landing deck, and quickly turned off the jets. I'd just flown up to a zeppelin! Wow! "Woo hoo!" I yelled.

The girls, far below me yelled, "Woo hoo!"

The door to the dis/embarkation lounge opened. "What is going on out here?" the purser stuck his head out. Now, his mouth fell open. "Where did you come from?"

I grinned. "Down there." I pointed down. Then I turned on the jets just a little and rose up about a foot into the air. "Bye!" I hovered there for a few moments.

I had to experiment a little with the nozzle controls to slowly descend back to the ground.

When I landed, Olivia couldn't seem to stop jumping up and down.

"I knew you could do it," Emma said, beaming.

"That was awesome!" Olivia said. "Awesome!"

"Wow! Neat!" Ava said, her usual reserve gone. "Wow."

The four of us smiled at each other for a moment. It was awesome to fulfill Mom's goal with my cohort, my sisters. "We did it together."

We all cheered. "Yay!"

Suddenly, Grandmother appeared in the doorway to the back-yard. "What is all this commotion, young ladies?"

I smiled. "I got it to work, Grandmother! I got Mom's jet-pack to work."

"Yeah," Olivia said. "She totally did. She just flew up to a zeppelin, and came back down."

"Yeah," Ava echoed. "She even landed on the deck and talked to the purser."

"It was wonderful," Emma said. "I knew she could do it. She's just like her mom."

I looked at Emma for a moment, blinking back tears.

"Really?" Grandmother put her hands over her heart. "I'm not sure I approve. That sounds dangerous Brittani. What if you got hurt?"

"It's not dangerous, Grandmother," I said. "Or don't you trust Mom? She knew what he was doing."

"I did trust your Mom. She was brilliant and wonderful." She put her hands down. "Can you show me?"

With Grandmother's help and Mom's old connections, I patented Mom's jet-pack technology. The jet-pack logo was a stylized picture of me and Emma in our Girl Guide uniforms. I thought it looked awesome. So did Emma.

The best part was the profits went to Girl Guides world-wide.

It was wonderful to think of girls like me (and Mom and Grand-mother) all over the world having the opportunity to meet and make true friends like Emma, Ava and Olivia--now and forever.

I knew Mom and Dad would be proud. Grandmother was defi-nitely proud. She'd actually cried and hugged me a long time when we opened the box with the first rocket-packs off the assembly line.

The 5-minute warning went off on my fon. "Oh no!" I shoved my fon in my pocket, ran to my room, grabbed my rocket-pack, ran down the hall and out the front door.

"Don't forget your Girl Guides uniform," Grandmother called after me.

"Got it!"

Once outside, I quickly powered up my rocket-pack and flew towards the zeppelin stop where I met up with Emma, Ava , and Olivia.

"Hi!" Olivia said.

"Morning!" Ava said.

"Great to see you!" Emma said.

The four of us turned and jetted for school.

Rocket-packs had become very popular.

Especially with girls.

ABOUT THE AUTHOR

Lesley L. Smith is a scientist with a Ph.D. in physics and a science fiction author with a M.F.A. in creative writing. Her stories have appeared in venues such as *Analog Science Fiction and Fact* and *Fiction River*. She's published eight novels including *The Quantum Cop*, *Conservation of Luck*, and *A Jack By Any Other Name*.

JETPACKS AND CYBERBRAINS

Jetpacks and Cyberbrains
A Star Minds Lone Wolves Team story
Barbara G. Tarn

Icy Aya controlled her breath as she jogged back to the house. Her brown ponytail danced behind her and she was sweating under the sun, but she didn't care. She had missed the green landscape after the flatness of Sylvania and the Gray Desert of Ulba'wis. Running outside was better than just going to the house gym, where sooner or later Jes-syd would show up.

Not that he spoke whenever he did. He just exercised next to her, but his simple presence was unsettling. So it was better going out for a run in the green valley of Vilas Lok she was starting to consider her new home away from home.

Well, there was no home to go back to anyway and the little house with its slanted roof was much better than her small apartment on Friport. She was on a real planet with real air and real gravity, not on an artificial world.

And she was surrounded by shielded minds, so she didn't need to raise her mental shields to the max. She had the dimmed telepathy of Friport with the fresh air of a real planet – like Marc'harid had been.

She pumped up the volume of her headphones when she saw her grandfather and his cousin were seated in their front garden. It was too late to change route, so she kept jogging, eyes to the ground, music pumping rhythm in her ears.

Iso-bel! Stop right now!

Her grandfather's telepathic order made her sigh and slow down in front of his house identical to hers. The two buildings had been constructed next to each other behind the bigger house of the owner of the valley, Hariel Reubel.

Icy Aya switched off her music player and kept jogging on the spot, to keep moving while she looked her grandfather in the eyes.

"Good morning," she grumbled. "I would like to continue to my own room and shower if you don't mind."

"I do mind," he replied. "I'm worried for you. Since when are you so active and always moving?"

She scoffed. "Since I was a hyperactive child," she replied. "There was no gym in Kay-low's house, so I went out running. The Sylvanian Academy and the Ulba'wissian school taught me how to stay fit."

"And why don't you use the house gym you requested here?" he asked with an amused smile.

She stopped her jog and scowled at him. "I enjoy running outside more. I'm using the house gym too. And it's none of your business, since I'm twenty-five and not even my father was like this!"

"Like what?" he asked innocently. "I told you, I'm worried for you. I think you're avoiding Jes-syd."

"What if I am? We're history!"

Her grandfather shook his head and sighed. "As stubborn as a Vaurabi," he said. "I'm the one who lost a love mind link. You're wasting your gift, Iso-bel."

"I don't want a love mind link with Jes-syd," she snapped,

putting her fists on her hips.

"Really?" He sounded teasing. "With Hariel maybe?"

"With nobody!" She growled and switched on the music again. "Good-bye!"

And she resumed jogging towards her house. She felt his laughter in her head. She couldn't fool her grandfather. But she didn't want to mind-link at the moment. With anyone.

Her grandfather's family had the gift of mind links that allowed two individuals to become one. It had made the family stand out on a planet of telepaths, but that planet had been destroyed five years earlier and there were very few survivors.

The mighty Sire telepaths who used to rule the galaxy were now a minority, scattered through the Star Nations. Her grandfather and his cousin. Jes-syd's mother. A few more lucky ones who either managed to get away from the dying planet or weren't on the planet itself at the time of the catastrophe.

Icy Aya had lost her parents and younger brother that day and hadn't been able to maintain the relationship with Jes-syd who had been spared because, like her, he was studying on another planet. Unlike their best friends, Ran-ald and Emma-lin, who had died on Marc'harid.

Heck, even Hariel was a survivor! A natural telepath whose parents came from Wega, he had married a Sire only to lose him in the cosmic catastrophe that had destroyed the former Imperial planet.

The only non-telepath in that valley was Shanell, her roommate at the Sylvanian Academy, who now had an artificial mind shield. Icy Aya had hoped her ex-boyfriend would settle on her ex-roommate, but apparently Jes-syd was still stuck on her and Shanell was more interested in Hariel.

She went straight to her spartan room to shower and changed into a pair of tight-fitting pants and her Indian embroidered shirt, a souvenir of her second trip to Gaia for her first official job – to kill an ambassador on the Galactic Showboat.

While she was in the kitchen to order something from the food dispenser, she heard Shanell coming in through the front door.

"Guys, we've got a job!"

Icy Aya grabbed her plate and a bottle of water, and headed for the living room where she found Shanell with Jes-syd and Hariel. Shanell was wearing one of her corsets, so she'd gone to Hariel's to do more than look for a job. Her bob of copper hair reached her shoulders, showing dark roots, but Icy Aya had managed to keep her away from hairdressers whenever they went to town.

Jes-syd looked mildly curious as he sat down and tucked a strand of his golden mane behind his ear. His amber eyes glanced at her before looking at Shanell and Hariel, who sat in an armchair to avoid having anyone sitting next to him.

Icy Aya took in the handsome forty-year-old with his hazel green eyes and taught muscles barely hidden under his shirt and pants. Sometimes she really wished she could be as open and extrovert as Shanell and ask him to have sex. Not in front of Jes-syd, of course. If only she could do a job alone with him...

She curled up in a corner of the couch while Jes-syd asked, "So, what have you got?"

"An anonymous government official needs a team to assassinate Hayden Smith, a security executive of Batya-Serova Communications, and recover their cyberbrainm" Shanell announced triumphantly.

"And we will need to acquire some special equipment first," Hariel added. "Jetpacks on New SETH World."

"Ah, so that's why you like the job," Jes-syd teased. "You get to go home – sort of!"

"My home world is as destroyed as yours," Hariel replied. "But yes, I'll be glad to go back to New SETH World. It's been some time since I was there."

"So we're going there with the Haiduc," Shanell said. "We get the jetpacks, then Aya can kill the guy and Hariel and Jes-syd recover the cyberbrain. How's that for teamwork?"

Icy Aya shrugged. "Fine by me."

She'd need the file on her victim before the actual killing. And probably some time to learn how to use a jetpack. She had tried one, a couple of times, at the Sylvanian Academy, but it had been three years since then and she must be reminded how those things worked.

She assumed she'd need a jetpack because the target had one too. And a cyberbrain, a mechanical casing for the human brain that allowed a mental interface with the meganet and other computer networks.

Jes-syd immediately ran a search on Hayden Smith. He had bronze eyes, dimples and blond hair. He loved blind faith and large cities. One of his hobbies was solving puzzles. And as security executive he had a jetpack and other smart-weapons that he controlled through his cyberbrain.

"He's had military training," Jes-syd said with a frown. "Maybe Hariel should help you."

"I will get a jetpack too," Hariel said. "But I'm not killing anyone. I'm a thief, not a killer." He looked at Icy Aya. "Although I look forward to the day when you won't be able to kill anymore either."

She looked away, frowning. It was hard to kill for telepaths. Unless their feelings and empathy were frozen by grief. Like hers.

Icy Aya tried not to think about Shanell's new starship's name. The Light Weight Starship didn't look like its namesake that had belonged to her father, so as long as she didn't think about the name, she was fine. In her mind, Shanell's starship was the Zodie 2, not the Haiduc.

She usually sat in the navigator's chair to keep her friend company, but this time she stayed in the passenger space to study her target. She should probably hit him when he was off work and out there with his jetpack. He seemed to enjoy flying around and shooting at animals in the wild. A weird kind of hunter that Icy Aya liked less and less. He might have a nice face and sweet smile, but she didn't like how he behaved.

"Can we control him through his implant?" she asked Jes-syd, remembering how she'd helped protect witnesses to a murder that had been committed remotely through a brain-computer interface implant. "Is the cyberbrain like BCIs?"

"Sort of but not completely," Jes-syd answered, thoughtful. He pursed his lips. "I don't think I can get in and shut it off, or I'd do it for you. That software is well protected and I wouldn't want to destroy it. They asked us to take it back intact."

"Right, so hacking it is out of the question," she muttered.

"I thought you'd be happy to get some action," Jes-syd said with a smile.

She glared at him, then shrugged. "I don't care. Whatever needs to be done."

Shanell's starship was fast and they reached New SETH World in no time. The Super Enhanced Trans Humanoids had transferred their labs from the space station that had given birth to Hariel to the smaller moon of Ulba'wis that had been hollowed out to host the scientists that had survived.

Hariel himself was enhanced since his nanotechnologist mother had given him a virtually invulnerable body to cure his frail frame. It had taken years to transform Hariel's body into a marvel of technology with decentralized circulatory systems, as well as a form of synthetic blood.

Nanobots could boost immune systems, helping to exterminate pathogens. They could also regulate blood pressure, or repair some of the damage caused by the aging process, or accelerate the healing of wounds.

Hariel had been a sickly boy and his mother had turned him into a healthy and strong man on SETH World before it was destroyed. A space station orbiting binary stars, it had ended its life ingloriously, as a fireball expanding at very high speed and vanishing in a blue-white flash, its fragments vaporized in the silent explosion, but Hariel and his mother had made it safely away and had ended up on Vilas Lok.

Icy Aya wasn't sure when Hariel had gone to New SETH World. Shanell had been there to get an exoskeleton for a job that she hadn't been able to keep. Jes-syd had wanted to go there since he had found out his mother was still alive in the recesses of the Vaurabi Labs of Marc'harid. Icy Aya was just curious.

Her father's bionic arm had come from the Vaurabi Labs, not SETH World. The Sire planet always had the most advanced technology, in fact her great-grandfather, the last emperor, hadn't liked the freedom of SETH World and tightly controlled whatever happened in the Vaurabi Labs.

As a telepath with an ESP mother, Icy Aya had never wished to augment her body, but she knew her late father's first girlfriend had survived the accident that had taken her father's arm with an artificial body that had been modified and remade on SETH World when the Vaurabi Labs were open to the whole galaxy and the empire was no more.

She didn't meet the ex, though. Izzy-lee worked in the exoskeleton department and they went straight to the jetpack department where a female technician showed to her and Hariel a couple of different models.

Eladia Hohstadt had silver dreadlocks and dark amber eyes. She wore a black suit and had a cybernetic arm. Her mind wasn't shielded, so Icy Aya could see that Eladia was zealous and amoral. But as long as Eladia gave her the right jetpack, she didn't care.

"Should we buy these?" she asked Hariel, frowning. "Can we rent them?"

"Is it possible to rent them?" Hariel asked Eladia. "We need them for a job, but not forever."

Eladia sighed. "I guess," she muttered. "Let me ask my boss."

Icy Aya tried on the smaller jetpack. She was shorter and

nimbler than Hariel who could carry a bigger weight. She didn't feel very comfortable and wondered how she could shoot her target while maneuvering the jetpack. Should she blow his mind like she had done with the ambassador?

Eladia came back with a price for rental and completed her instructions, allowing them to try the jetpacks in a vast underground room.

"It looks funny," Shanell commented when they went back to the starship with the special equipment. "Although I prefer having a starship around my body when I fly!"

Icy Aya shrugged. She was still worried about how to shoot while controlling the jetpack. Her target obviously used his cyberbrain to control the jetpack, so he had his hands free to shoot.

"We could use them to fly to where he is," Hariel suggested. "Those jetpacks are more discreet than a starship. We land in the vicinity and then proceed on foot. You can be a sniper, I take it?"

"Yes," she snapped. She always had 10/10 at target practice.

They had a quick meal at the canteen of New SETH World that had better food dispensers than the starship, then they went back on the Haiduc to head for Alahairo where Hayden Smith lived and worked.

Icy Aya checked her duffel bag and her weapons. She could forget her black alloy swords, but she should take her smart-gun as well as her shotgun.

"Can you shoot?" she asked Hariel.

He shook his head. "I'm afraid it wasn't part of my training," he answered with a smile. "And I never owned a gun."

She nodded with a grunt. She could do it alone. Hariel was just backup.

Batya-Serova Communications had its headquarters in Alahairo's main town, so Shanell landed at the main spaceport. The planet of traders was terraformed but mostly a huge cemetery with only a few towns scattered here and there. There was even a Galaxy Police space station in orbit around the planet, so they'd have to be careful not to get caught in the act.

They took adjoining rooms at a hotel in town to study the situation and their target. Hariel seemed to know where most security cameras were in town, but they had decided they wouldn't commit their crime too close to the company building – a skyscraper that seemed to tower over any other building.

Hayden Smith went out of town on his day off every five days. He lived alone in a condo on the outskirts of the city and practiced his hobby alone. He said he was doing it to keep the cemeteries free of wild animals messing with the tombs, but nobody had officially appointed him to do the job.

The guardians of the cemeteries let him shoot at whatever he fancied, as long as he removed the corpses. Most of his kills weren't really edible, but he took many furs and hides, and then he resold them to one of the factories of the planet, making some money on the side.

The anonymous government official who had hired them wasn't happy with his hobby and the unpaid taxes on his extra earnings, therefore he wanted Smith dead, possibly making it look like an accident.

"We could get to his hunting zone with the jetpacks and you could shoot him," Hariel suggested as they studied the map of the city and its surroundings the next morning.

It had been a good night of sleep for everyone except Icy Aya, but she wasn't going to show her weakness. She finished her second cup of coffee watching the others comment on the map on Jes-syd's tablet screen in their rooms.

Sometimes Smith took his flying car and went farther, but lately he'd been hunting close enough to his home to allow them to get there with the jetpacks. There were no roads through the cemeteries, therefore one either had a flying car or a jetpack.

Icy Aya pursed her lips, frowning at the map. "I see no place where I could hide and aim," she grumbled. "If he sees me, he'll shoot me first!"

"How about this chapel?" Jes-syd enlarged a part of the map on his screen.

They zoomed in to the satellite view and saw it was a mausoleum or a cenotaph where one could crouch and be hidden from the sky. There were trees planted among the tombs, but they didn't offer enough cover.

"A chapel or a mausoleum might be a good place to set up an ambush," Hariel said. "See if there's anything closer to the edge of the cemetery, on the side of that forest that probably hides all the animals that visit it."

"Should we aim for the forest itself?" Icy Aya suggested. "Those trees are good enough to cover me."

"We don't know how close he gets to the forest when he hunts," Hariel replied. "The guardian's home is also on that side, because there's a river that runs around those hills, so I doubt he gets anywhere too close."

"How do we make sure he goes to that cemetery tomorrow?" Shanell asked, worried. "You could go there in the morning, but what if he doesn't show up?"

"That's why you're here to keep an eye on him," Hariel replied. "If you see him headed somewhere else, you call us and we follow."

Icy Aya went to the roof terrace of the hotel with Hariel. This time she had slept, albeit with the help of pills. Her grandfather said she had PTSD, but she didn't think so. Although she still dreamed of the dreadful day her parents had cut the blood mind link with her to vanish forever.

They both donned their jetpacks and she put her shotgun on her shoulder while he had a pouch where he put his tablet. The wind was strong on the tenth floor but the jetpacks were powerful enough to take them against it. They both wore closed helmets for the flight anyway. Those things could go quite fast.

They took off and the jetpacks kept them up, flying towards the outskirts of the city and beyond. Icy Aya had seen the cemeteries on Marc'harid – before it was destroyed – with monuments made of marble, granite or similar materials that rose vertically above the ground. She had seen plenty of monumental cemeteries also on Gaia.

Alahairo was different, though. There were some older mausoleums or cenotaphs, but mostly it was a rural cemetery that turned into a natural cemetery where people were buried with or without coffins directly in the ground.

Wildlife proliferated in the rural cemeteries that used landscaping in a park-like setting. They featured well-planned walkways which gave extensive access to graves and planned plantings of trees, bushes, and flowers.

And the newer parts had no fences and simply melted into the countryside, eco-cemeteries where natural burials – motivated by a desire to be environmentally conscious with the body rapidly decomposing and becoming part of the natural environment without incurring the environmental cost of traditional burials – filled the land.

Those two bigger sections had no places where one could hide, though. Hence Icy Aya and Hariel had selected a lone chapel at the edge of the monumental part to land and hide in, waiting for Smith to show up. It was also surrounded by a graveyard that could give additional protection.

The chapel had a broken door and it was very ruined inside. The names of the family members interred there were unreadable. Traces of a fresco still decorated the walls high up near the ceiling. It was quite dark inside, and the dust of years gone by made Icy Aya sneeze at first.

The family was probably extinct and nobody cared about that

chapel anymore. The tiled roof had holes and mold was slowly invading the burial space along with timid plants that gave touches of green near the narrow windows by the door.

They put down the jetpacks and helmets, and Hariel sat on the dirty floor to check if there was a signal. His tablet connected to the guardian's house and he was able to see their target reaching the cemetery before they actually heard his jetpack.

Icy Aya, who was looking over his shoulder, grabbed her shotgun. Smith was on the other side of the chapel, so she went out, lying low behind bushes and grave stones, trying to see him, guided by the noise of his jetpack.

Looking around the corner of the wall of the chapel, she finally saw him, but immediately ducked, since he was turned her way. She saw his blast hit something in front of her and flattened herself even more as he approached to grab whatever he had shot.

She was glad of her petite and willowy build that allowed her to hide behind the statue of an old tomb to watch him. He landed and leaned to grab something. She took aim. He straightened, holding a hare by its ears. She waited. He put the corpse in a bag and took off again. Her viewfinder kept following him.

As soon as he was off the ground and with his back to her, she pulled the trigger, hitting the jetpack and sending him spiraling down with a scream. "Yes!" she whispered, rising and jogging to where he had crashed.

He was still alive, but badly wounded. She took her smart-gun and finished him. Pull the trigger and don't think. A mechanical action, ingrained in years of training.

She felt Hariel's presence when he put a hand on her shoulder. "I'll get the cyberbrain," he said.

She waited, frowning. They should blow up the jetpack so that whoever found the body wouldn't know he'd been shot.

Hariel stepped back with the metal cap and gently slid it into his pouch. She kicked the body to make it roll on its face, then backed away until she almost lost sight of her victim.

"Stand back," she told Hariel.

She aimed carefully and was almost deafened by the sudden explosion of the jetpack, but she was far enough from it not to be affected. The fire quickly subsided since he had fallen in a rocky spot. The charred remnants of their target would show no traces of the job.

She went back to the chapel to retrieve her own equipment.

"You are truly icy, Aya," Hariel said, serious.

They were alone. It was her only chance. The other two wouldn't know.

"Melt me," she replied, putting down her weapons. "You know you can, Wonder Man."

He smiled. "I don't think so, little sister."

She scowled. "I'm not your sister! You didn't have qualms with Shanell, did you?"

"Shanell is not a telepath," he answered. "I am used to non-telepath lovers. With my husband it was different."

"Sire kisses. Mouth and mind. I know exactly what you mean."

"And would a Sire kiss be enough for you, Iso-bel Aya Shermac?" he asked, amused. "I'm fifteen years older than you. I could almost be your father."

And he towered over her like her late father had. Her heart thundered in her chest. She wanted a Sire kiss. She wanted to see his mind, if only for a moment. A blissful moment, surely.

"I don't care how old you are. Yes, I want a Sire kiss."

"I'm sorry, not going to happen," he replied with a mock bow.

"Why, because you think I'm an icy, heartless Sire?" she snapped.

"No, because there are parts of me I'm not ready to share with anyone," he answered patiently. "You can have sex, if it's what you want, but no Sire kisses."

"Did you have a mind link with your husband?"

"No, or I wouldn't have survived. I'm not as tough as your grandfather."

"Leave my grandfather out of this!" she snapped. "I'm twenty-five, I don't need his permission to do anything! I don't need to be looked after! I'm a hitwoman and a mercenary!"

He chuckled. "Yes, we know, Icy Aya, you're a professional. And you should know one shouldn't mix work and personal relationships. We're a team, I'm your teammate. We can have sex, but nothing more."

"I hope you're not doing this for Jes-syd," she grumbled, grabbing her jetpack and putting it on her shoulders. Helmet. Shotgun. Her heart still thundering. Her mind still ready to take down a few shields and show her true self to the handsome man.

"Actually, I'm doing it for you," he replied. "I'm a criminal, wanted by the GP." His hazel green eyes were teasing her again. She glared at him and stormed out of the chapel, switching on the jetpack to get back to the hotel.

Mr. H was dead for the galaxy. And he'd been a thief and a fraudster, not a killer. Like her. She knew he didn't want her because she was a killer. Maybe even Jes-syd would be repulsed if she showed him how coldly she had killed someone. She felt no remorse. Nothing.

Only the wish to nestle against Hariel and let him cuddle her until the end of time.

"Are you all right?" Jes-syd asked, worried.

"Yes," she snapped. "Take that damn cyberbrain to the official and let's get out of here."

"We need to get paid and take the jetpacks back to New SETH World," Shanell said, unhappy.

"Stay here and relax, ladies, we'll take care of everything," Hariel said.

Icy Aya couldn't relax. She had to keep moving. She went to the hotel gym and exercised until she was so tired she collapsed back in her room and slept until dinner time.

Shanell shook her awake and they went downstairs together to meet with Jes-syd and Hariel.

"We got paid. We got a bonus. The GP found the body and classified it as an accident," Hariel announced, raising his glass of fruit juice. "We only need to refuel and take the jetpacks back."

"Good," Icy Aya grumbled. "Maybe you should dump me on Friport on the way back to Vilas Lok."

"Why?" Jes-syd looked panicked.

"You don't need me in this team any more than I need you guys to find work," she answered bluntly.

Hariel took her hand across the table. "We need you, Iso-bel. We're a team of lone wolves, but we need each other."

"We need someone military-trained like you!" Shanell added eagerly.

"We need your strength and determination," Jes-syd added. "We're not a complete team without you."

"Each of us has different skills." Hariel let go of her hand. "And we can take it to the next level of professionalism if we stick together. Do you want me to go back to stealing for the thrill of it so you can come after me again to cash a bounty?"

"Hariel..." She scowled and he shot her an impish smile.

"You're one of us, Iso-bel, Icy Aya or whatever you want to be called. We're not giving up on you."

But you wouldn't give me a Sire kiss. You're not taking down your mind shields.

She transmitted only to him. He transmitted back an image of himself much younger, dressed all in black and all bloodied.

My mother died here his mind added. *In my arms. I couldn't save her. Is this enough to make you stay?*

She gulped and slowly nodded, losing herself in his hazel green eyes. Jes-syd exhaled in relief, oblivious to the telepathic conversation and Shanell patted her shoulder.

"Thank you, Aya. Glad you're still with us," she said cheerfully.

Icy Aya looked away from Hariel and finished her meal in silence.

🕸

As they left New SETH World again to head back for Vilas Lok, they saw a cyborg space whale, listening to microwave transmissions not far from the hollowed moon.

"Doesn't she look familiar?" Jes-syd asked, as Shanell zoomed in on the strange sight. "Iso-bel, remember when we were on Gaia?"

Icy Aya stood behind him, leaning on the back of his seat. She'd been watching the cachalot too, trying to remember where she had seen it.

"Dubai beach," she whispered. "When we went skinny dipping."

Jes-syd beamed. "Yes! And she ended up on the beach waiting to be taken home!"

"And she was taken home..." She pondered. "And they turned her into a cyborg space whale?"

"Let's see if I can contact her." Jes-syd turned to the comm under Shanell's amused stare. Hariel watched them from the bottom of the cockpit, mildly curious.

Jes-syd managed to get through the microwaves, and the sperm whale answered back in the same way, with the starship's computer translating for its human occupants. On Gaia they had used telepathy, but it was harder to do it in space and locked inside a starship.

At eighteen Jes-syd and Iso-bel had traveled to Gaia and while sitting on the beach to dry themselves in the cooling air of the night, a solitary sperm whale had stopped by to say hello. She was old and tired, but she had offered to take them to their hotel under the sea on her back.

They had asked her why she had wandered into the Persian Gulf, and she had answered she was going home. She had deposited them at the hotel's pier and as soon as she was stranded, a beam hit her and she vanished.

Now, seven years later, she confirmed her rendezvous with a starship orbiting Gaia who had taken her home where she'd been enhanced and could now wander in space as if it were the ocean. She was still old and tired and didn't care when her life ended, as long as it was among the stars. She'd been stuck on a planet way too long.

Jes-syd was thoughtful on the way back. The cachalot had decided to die among the stars and they were still mourning the loss of their home planets. "Maybe we should be more like Shanell, eager to travel and see other places..."

"You haven't traveled much," Icy Aya grumbled. "And you don't own a starship."

"The Vision is yours," Hariel said. "When we get back, I'll make sure to add your biometrics to her mainframe. Although we live on the pleasure planet, where most people spend their holidays and vacations..."

"And where do the locals go to see something new?" Shanell asked, amused.

"On cruises or the Galaxy Express," he answered. "I have traveled quite a lot myself..."

"To go stealing on different planets," Jes-syd teased. "No more Mr. H, though, remember?"

Hariel chuckled. "Of course. And we have the best starship pilot in the Star Nations to take us around now."

"Are you making a fool of me?" Shanell demanded, pretending to be outraged.

"I would never dare upset our beloved captain," he answered with a mock bow.

Icy Aya smiled despite herself while the others burst out laughing. At least Jes-syd had stopped thinking about that trip to Gaia, when they were still together, before the catastrophe. And Hariel was right, they were a good team. She should overcome her grumpiness and enjoy their company from now on.

ABOUT THE AUTHOR

Barbara G. Tarn had an intense life in the Middle Ages that stuck to her through the centuries. She prefers swords to guns, long gowns to mini-skirts, and even though she buried the warrior woman, she deplores the death of knights in shining chainmail. She likes to think her condo apartment is a medieval castle, unfortunately lacking a dungeon to throw noisy neighbors and naughty colleagues in.

The story in this anthology belongs to her Star Minds futuristic universe, a science fantasy saga. She's a writer, sometimes artist, mostly a world-creator and story-teller. Two of her stories received an Honorable Mention at the Writers of the Future contest. She writes, draws, ignores her day job and blogs at: http://creativebarbwire.wordpress.com.

For more info on the series or other titles of Unicorn Productions join the mailing list and receive the bi-monthly newsletter to be notified of new releases, sales and other author's news and the exclusive opportunity to get free stories or discounts on Barbara G.Tarn's works.

CAPTAIN VIRTUE AND THE LEAGUE OF EVIL

R.G. Hart

RED increased power to the twin thrusters of the rocket pack as they approached the dirigible visible through the thin cloud cover just below them at four thousand feet.

There was a high probability they were about to experience a fiery death—well, Virtue would die of course but not RED. The dangerous high-speed approach was to demonstrate they were not adverse to use courage, disregard for personal safety, and adaptability when under the pressure of a deadline. They needed this contract. Badly. Virtue needed to eat and she needed a new supply of radioactive isotopes.

"Hey, RED, watch it," Virtue said over the comm in his flight helmet. "Isn't this a little fast?"

"Don't worry, Virtue, trust me."

"Okay," His deep baritone sounded apprehensive, but since he wasn't the brightest star in the heavens. RED was certain Virtue would do whatever RED told him. More importantly the pilot had signed an unbreakable contract ten years ago. Wherever RED goes so goes Captain Virtue.

The sensors said they were now within fifty yards of the fast moving air ship. The sensors also showed the coordinates of door they would use to enter that ship. RED adjusted their course slightly and prepared for the approach maneuver. Timing must be perfect or the virtual recorders wouldn't have the images he wanted the military brass to see. An exploding rocket pack and a dirigible crashing to the ground entombed in a boiling fireball wouldn't do much for their credibility. Drama is everything when it comes to show biz, RED's father often says. Maybe a little too often but that's a whole other issue in itself.

"We have arrived," said Virtue as they hovered in the air next to the door of the dirigible's passenger cabin. Three pairs of eyes covered by goggles stared back at them from the windows lining the passenger cabin a look of astonishment on their faces.

Perfect, thought RED. Surprise is an art form when practiced by a virtuoso.

RED transmitted an override signal to unlock the door and prepared to enter the passenger cabin. "Virtue, have your blaster ready."

"Roger wilco."

"Don't use those words, Virtue. We talked about this." Moron. RED rolled her visual receptors as if they were real human eyes.

"Sorry...blaster locked and loaded..." RED made a note to have another talk with Virtue about communication etiquette. This was getting old. Hopefully the potential clients wouldn't notice her partners' faux pas.

The goggled crewmembers of the dirigible had finally sprung into action and were preparing to repel them. RED sensed they were now armed and had their projectile weapons aimed at the door ready for the assault. "Virtue, place a mini bomb on the door." Without thankfully saying anything Virtue took a mini bomb from a sleeve on his utility belt then pressed the magnetized strip located on one side of the small explosive device to the steel door. The wind whipped at his leather flight jacket.

RED activated the rocket pack's maneuvering jets to move them far enough away from the door so the blast wouldn't affect them then triggered the weapon. The bomb blew the door in accompanied by a shower of sparks and a loud thump audible over then the wind. Acrid smoke billowed out from the passenger cabin swept away by the force of the rushing air at this altitude. The twin external rocket engines on the dirigible were still running and Red could register the heat. They needed to avoid going near the exhaust ports of the powerful engines.

"Hold on. We're going in fast. Prepare to fire at any moving target."

"Okay, RED." Virtue responded his tone sharp and focused.

A hint of doubt occurred to RED suggested by previous experience. "Set your weapon on stun, Virtue, we don't need another Toledo." He didn't respond but she knew he understood. The last thing they needed were multiple fatalities as they did in that dead end bar outside the Ohio city when Virtue in a panic fired his weapon into a crowd of angry bikers.

The external sensors had guided them to the perfect spot to enter the smoky interior of the passenger cabin without being in the line of fire of any of the crewmembers inside. If they only have external sensors how do they see what's inside? Confusing Virtue had engaged the infrared feature in his flight helmet and had his blaster out of its holster in his right hand at the ready. RED cut power to the thrusters as they shot through the blasted door of the cabin. The whine power down of the rocket pack's motor echoed in the enclosed space of the cabin after they were shut down.

Once inside one of the crew persons stumbled out of the smoke in front of them covered head to toe in dark soot. He or she—the voluminous uniform and leather helmet, plus the goggles obscuring the eyes, made it impossible to determine the gender—sagged to the knees and fell forward striking the deck with a loud slap then lay still. The projectile weapon the crewmember had been holding skidded across the deck toward them.

"I'm reading two more crew near the flight control panel straight ahead." Red paused to double check the readings. "They're out cold. Everyone's alive but unconscious."

"Great," Virtue said proudly holstering his blaster. "Captain Virtue wins again."

"Really?" RED said sarcastically.

After they shut down the dirigibles engines they drifted until two Navy Special Service dirigibles, plus two F9.9 jet fighters, acting as escorts, arrived to extract the unconscious crew and retrieve the payload. Then the enemy dirigible would be towed to the ocean to be destroyed in a ball of flame by air-to-air missiles. The airships remains would land in the sea and disappear in the shifting tides. To hell with the environmentalists, thought RED.

After RED attended a debriefing session without Virtue, pilots were unnecessary at debriefs, they arrived back at their sixth floor headquarters—located in an abandoned six story office building in the middle of a bad part of town—Virtue sighed wearily then dropped into one the three cigarette scarred oak chairs in the office. A heavy steel desk sat in the middle of the room, three of the walls were lined with military gray steel filing cabinets. The only saving grace was the two open windows facing the street far below allowed a cool breeze to provide relief from the odors of mold and rot that filled the room. The breeze was welcome but the traffic noise rising from the busy street wasn't.

Of course none of this really bothered RED as an AI rocket pack but she did need to provide some creature comforts for her one employee and front man. The contract between them was clear on this point.

Virtue undid the leather strap under his chiseled chin then

slipped off his helmet letting it drop to the floor next to the chair with a thump. He then began undoing the buttons of his rust colored leather-flying jacket after he had taken off his heat resistant leather gloves and slapped them on the desk.

"Man, RED, I'm beat. That was a hell of a mission." He ran one hand through his thick, wavy blond hair and closed his eyes as he eased back against the chair back.

"Yeah, I know, kid, but we had to make an impression for the Imperial staff."

Virtue snorted without opening his eyes. He crossed his arms over his wide chest. "What was the payload aboard that dirigible anyway, anything interesting?"

RED made a snort sound that matched Virtue's. "Not that it matters but I'm told it was two crates of fresh pineapples destined for a drug lord on Papaola Island."

"What about the drug lord?" Virtue asked as if he was interested which RED knew he wasn't.

"I don't know they didn't share that detail with me."

"What did they say about our performance?" Virtue responded getting right to the important part of RED's meeting with the brass.

"They liked what they saw but they said they still have us and another team in mind. We seem to be in a tie with LARP and Commander Heroic."

Virtue dropped his arms and his eyes popped open as a scowl spread across his handsome features like a tidal wave. The chair creaked as he sat forward. His azure eyes had an intensity in them RED rarely saw in Virtue. The guy was suddenly lit up by a display of passion something he hadn't displayed in a very long time. What had triggered this did he really want this contract so bad?

"What's up, Virtue? We've been in competition for contracts many times why should this be any different? You're freaking me out."

Before he could respond a delivery truck on the street below ground its gears and began blasting its air horn. This was followed by a prolonged screech of multiple brakes being applied then the impact of metal-on-metal and shattering glass. The cacophony of sound echoing around the small office made conversation impossible.

RED turned her visual interface toward the windows in time to see a haze of smoke drift upward. Virtue's shoulders had eased but he appeared preoccupied not the least bit interested in what was happening outside. He normally loved a good accident.

Finally after what seemed like an eternity the noise began to ebb until there were only shouts and the sounds of flesh and bone striking each other. In the distance the sirens of the emergency responders began to gradually build in intensity. They didn't have much time.

"Virtue, tell me what's wrong. I really need to know."

He'd been lost in thought but her question broke through his pondering. He shifted his gaze to RED and emitted a soft snort of derisiveness. "Mandy Heroic," he said between gritted teeth.

"What about her?"

He rolled his eyes and there was a brief flash of regret across his handsome features. "Mandy and I go way back. We were in flight school together. We were rivals. Veterans. Competitors..." His words trailed off and a scowl marred his forehead as his eyes became even more intense. "She died," he whispered.

Red was stunned into silence. They'd worked together for almost twenty years ever since she had come off the assembly line at the Wright Brothers Rocket Factory. He was the only pilot she'd ever had. Until now she always considered their relationship as good friends who shared everything about their pasts. Well, at least she'd shared everything. Virtue had apparently been reluctant to share a few wrinkles from his past.

Hold on. "Who died?" she finally asked. The sirens were growing louder now. Soon the screaming fire trucks, cop cars, and ambulances would converge on the neighborhood to overwhelm their conversation.

"My girlfriend, Elsa..." His jaw locked, as the words died away his eyes overflowed with tears that spilled down his ruddy stubble covered cheeks.

Red considered the foreign sounding name for a second. "Who was she?"

"My flight instructor...and Heroic's too."

Time was fast growing short the blare of the sirens was getting closer. "Tell me."

Virtue sucked in a deep breath then let it out slowly before launching into his story. He had leaned forward in the chair his head hanging his arms resting on his thighs.

"It was just before our first solo...me, Heroic, and the five other students who hadn't washed out." The pilot academy had a high failure rate for new wanta be pilots.

Virtue continued. "Elsa had run through all our ground checks with us to ensure we fully understood the importance of checking over your aircraft before taking off. I did mine perfectly." He shrugged. "Heroic not so much. She missed a few things either intentionally or in error I don't know. Anyway Elsa was furious. She'd been pounding these procedures into us for weeks. She tore a strip off Heroic in front of us students and the ground support crew."

"I gather Mandy Heroic didn't take this well?" said RED. Virtue shook his head. "So how did Elsa die? Did Mandy seek revenge for the humiliation?" RED had just entered the land of speculation.

Virtue lifted his head to peer at RED's visual receptors. She was shocked when he shook his head again. No? I must be missing something.

"She didn't die or wasn't Mandy seeking revenge? Which is it?"

"Elsa died alright in a plane crash the next day. The official report said it was a training accident. Elsa had taken Mandy up to test her on a few things prior to her attempting the solo again. It was Mandy's last chance or she'd wash out of the academy."

Now Red was really becoming puzzled. "But I thought you said Heroic killed Elsa?"

Virtue stared at her his eyes wide. "Huh, no, Heroic didn't kill Elsa it was an accident. I just told you, the official report—"

"Oh, for God's sake, Virtue," RED interrupted the pilot, "you said you didn't like Mandy. You were angry at her."

Virtue shrugged. "I don't like her sure but she didn't kill anyone. How did you get that idea?"

"You...Elsa died...Mandy embarrassed her...." RED stopped. "Oh, forget it."

The comm unit on the desk signaled there was a call coming in ending their inane conversation. Thank you. RED opened the comm link. "Go for RED."

"Admiral Roosevelt here. We've made our decision. You and Captain Virtue have earned the right to be part of the contract. We thought your performance capturing that rogue delivery ship was excellent."

Red considered the Admiral's choice of words. Something smelled bad like rotten grapefruit. She'd never eaten grapefruit, or any fruit actually, but her aroma sensors had certainly smelled the pungent acidic fruit. It wasn't the most pleasant of odors. She could well imagine when it rotted it was really stinky.

"Why only part of the mission? I thought the contract was for the entire mission, from start to finish."

"Well we thought two teams would be better able to infiltrate the League of Evil's security and bring back the proof we need confirming the existence of their death camps."

Death camps? There wasn't anything in the submission package about death camps. She assumed the mission was a standard seek and destroy. Meaning they would get in quietly take out an ammunition stockpile or some new secret weapon then escape hopefully in one piece. But never assume is the first lesson of any mission. This was going to be very high-risk.

The LOE would do everything they could to stop the information about their death camps from getting out. Maybe Admiral Roosevelt was right. Maybe two teams were better than one. Spread the risk out a little as it were.

RED rechecked the sensors something she never did on a normal mission but this pincher movement with LARP and Commander Heroic to the south of the LOE command facility and her and Virtue to the north was far from the usual assault plan.

Since she and LARP both had a personal protective shielding system and could outmaneuver just about anything that flew they would hopefully survive to fly another day. The two pilots were a different matter but in the world of freelance espionage they were considered expendable. The problem she faced was Red considered Virtue a friend and as far from expendable as a human being could get. She wasn't about to cross the imaginary line to unacceptable risk if it meant something might to happen to Virtue.

She had worked closely with LARP to devise, revise, and revise again a plan of attack until they both thought it stood the best chance of succeeding. Of course in any mission there were always unforeseen variables such as that darned human factor or human error. Humans too often had an unpredictable side of their natures that artificial intelligences had yet to crack. LARP would take the lead on the mission. No way was RED about to get into a who-has-the-biggest-rocket fight.

RED suggested they leave behind both pilots but LARP dismissed the idea without hesitation. He felt they would need the manual dexterity of a human being to rifle the files once they located them in the vast complex. His reasoning was hard to argue with so she agreed.

They attempted to pinpoint the location of the files they were after but they'd only managed to narrow it down to three possible locations. Three locations two teams. It made RED think maybe the Admiral should have hired three teams but two would have to do. It was a good thing the other team was led by LARP. He was by all reports a capable AI and very intuitive. She knew his reputation, but had never worked with him before this mission.

The weeks of preparation and planning made her a little more comfortable with him and Heroic, but in this business there were never any absolutes. It was just after midnight local time.

"Readings?" said LARP over the ghost comm. They were using a specially designed stealth communications interface manufactured by the Ford Corporation. Ford made weapons systems so why not comm systems?

"I'm showing six regiments of troopers, numerous weapons signatures including pulse rifles and seventeen air defense laser cannons." She paused to consider what a properly aimed laser canon could do to her external housing. If the housing ruptured all that would be left of them would be a cloud of radioactive dust. And everything both living and inanimate within five miles of the blast would be vaporized. She dismissed the vision of being engulfed in an atomic furnace. Her defensive shielding would protect her provided the laser wasn't a type they hadn't seen before. And since weapons development was evolving with each passing day however remote is always a possibility.

There were too many unknowns in this operation. She would have preferred six months of intelligence gathering before embarking on such a risky assault on an advanced LOE facility.

"I'm going to drop Heroic at site A," said LARP, "then proceed to site B. You and Virtue enter the complex at site C." Three red blinking lights appeared on the heads up display in Virtue's helmet after LARP transmitted the coordinates of the three entry points. RED made note of their assigned entry site on the map in her memory core.

Soon they were within fifty yards and so far there hadn't been any reaction by the defenses. "We good?" Virtue asked his whisper tense.

"So far, so good," she replied. The sensors showed the thickness of the door was ten times the other two sites. Now it made sense why LARP assigned them as a team to this location. Unfortunately they wouldn't be able to use mini-bombs to blow the door unless they used so many it would attract too much attention. Sensors indicated the lock was the most vulnerable point.

"We're coming in for a landing next to the door." RED reduced power to the thrusters as they moved to within twenty yards then cut the main thrusters and used the maneuvering jets to land them on the cement platform next to the door. The whine of the rocket motors died before they landed in a cloud of dust particles stirred up by the exhaust on the jets.

"We're shut down," RED said. Virtue acknowledged. He had his blaster in his right hand. He had set it to lethal force. She agreed with LARP they needed to apply lethal force against LOE troopers, the enemy wouldn't show mercy so why should they.

"Set your blaster on maximum, narrow beam, aim at the lock. We need to get inside a-sap." Virtue nodded he understood. RED activated the ghost comm. "Team Two landed at site C." LARP acknowledged the signal but oddly didn't report his and Heroic's positions. Team One had deviated from the agreed upon plan.

Something didn't feel right about these anomalies but RED had no evidence to suggest the mission was compromised so she decided to proceed. She redirected some of her internal power to external sensors. Extreme caution would be her mission protocol from this point forward.

She needed to focus. "Fire," she ordered.

Virtue pressed the firing stud on his blaster and a ruby red beam of concentrated energy shot from the business end of the weapon and struck the lock. The steel composite quickly glowed yellow then red then orange. Her sensors registered the sharp increase in heat until the locking mechanism began to melt as if it were made of pudding. Virtue released the firing stud and the beam ended. He then lifted his leg and kicked in the door with his booted foot. The door swung violently inward with a loud bang. Beyond the doorway was inky blackness. There were no lights.

Caution, thought RED. "Let's go. Activate your external lights."

Virtue, the blaster pistol still held ready to fire, tapped the interface on his right brass armband covering his leather jacket and the lights on his helmet lit up. They were bright enough to illuminate an area fifty feet in circumference.

Cautiously Virtue entered the facility his boot steps echoing in the quiet. Red thought she could hear his heart beat. Her sensors detected his heart rate was up and his breathing more forced. Blood pressure and adrenaline were normal for a combat situation. He was sweating evidenced by the increase in body heat under his uniform and the helmet. Of course the presence of water molecules on his skin confirmed the other indicators.

The helmet lights lit up the corridor the right side lined with closed doors as far as the light extended. Virtue stepped up to the first of the doors. The pine door was painted steel gray and there was a plaque affixed to it that read Communications.

Without being urged Virtue moved on to the next door. The plaque read Supply. They moved to the third door and found what they were looking for. The plaque read Administration. Hopefully the records detailing the death camps would be easy to find but somehow RED doubted it would be that simple.

Virtue tried the door handle but it was not surprisingly locked. "Hold on," RED instructed and Virtue hesitated shooting the lock as he had done with the exterior door. "I'll run a full sensor scan. The door may be alarmed or booby trapped."

As she ran the detailed scans Virtue undid the chest strap of the brown leather harness holding the rocket pack in place then loosened the shoulder straps. He slipped the straps off his shoulders then set RED on the floor next to him. He took careful aim at the lock both hands gripping the pistol stock waiting for the order to fire.

RED processed the incoming sensor data and determined the door was neither alarmed nor booby-trapped. "Okay."

Virtue fired and again the brilliant red beam of concentrated energy melted the lock. After he stopped firing he tapped the door open with his booted toe of his boot. The door swung in. The room beyond was shrouded in darkness. Virtue stepped in and felt along the wall until he found the light switch. He tapped the wall plate and the lights in the room flickered to life illuminating the interior.

He stepped inside his blaster still out. After disappearing for several seconds he reappeared to grab RED by the straps and carried her into the room. He set her on one of the four large oak desks in the center of the room. They were grouped together at the center of the expansive room. The walls were lined with army green filing cabinets and inside those were two additional rows of the same filing cabinets.

This was going to take far more time than they had to sort through. "Virtue, are there labels on the cabinets?"

He shut down the external lights on his helmet then took it off placing it on the desk next to RED. He moved the closest filing cabinet. "Yes, but they are numbers. They must have a numbered filing system. And the cabinets are locked. They require keys." He hesitated unsure what to do next.

RED thought for a few minutes. She recalled a man she once knew named Dewy. He invented numbered filing system used in offices around the world. The Imperial Armed forces had even adopted the system and the military was usually the most resistant to change. Not that it made much difference but a numbered system was going to be a serious challenge without a Rosetta stone to decipher what information pertained to what number.

Her visual receptors shifted to look at Virtue when he grunted. "Say maybe one of these desks has a file list?" he suggested.

"Good idea," RED replied impressed her pilot had come up with such an obvious idea. "Start looking," she urged him.

Virtue moved to each desk and searched them opening all the drawers and rifling through the contents. There were used paper sacks that once held a workers lunch, papers with written instructions, memos from superiors, pencils, pens, metal clips for holding papers together, telephone directories and other common office materials. But nothing that looked like a file list. Finally in the last desk Virtue discovered a metal ring crowded with keys. They were small keys obviously not for doors but for the filing cabinets. But which one was for which cabinet.

We're moving like molasses on a cold day, thought RED bitterly. Her father and creator had been right on with that saying. Winston Nemostat had been a genius in so many ways. It was at times like this she most missed his wise counsel.

How were they going to find the right cabinet? It would take far too long to check every key never mind having to review each file in each cabinet. They could get lucky however she wasn't about to depend on dumb luck.

It wouldn't be long before their intrusion would be discovered. They hadn't encountered any guards but that couldn't last. Time was growing short.

A sudden beep from the ghost comm broke through her deliberations. "Team Two."

"This is Team One. Evacuate site ASAP." The signal ended.

Had something gone wrong? Not that it mattered. They had to leave, now. "Okay, Virtue, let's wind it up. We're outta here."

Suddenly Virtue had his blaster pistol aimed at her a sardonic grin on his handsome features. His blue eyes reflected scorn. What was happening?

"What are you doing, Willie?" she said using his first name something she rarely did.

He arched one eyebrow and stepped out of range of her onboard defensive systems. The electro shock nodes and stun gas ejector tubes built into her frame could take out an enemy within a range of two feet. This prevented any non-authorized person from gaining control of her.

"I need to delay your departure," he said grimly as the grin melted from his eyes and lips.

"Why?"

When he didn't reply instead scanned the room his pistol remaining aimed at her it occurred to her he was taking orders from someone other than her. If he triggered the blaster her personal shields would hold for a few minutes at this range but once the thin beam of energy pierced the protective field her tanks would rupture. Their deaths would be quick, but she suspected that wasn't the end game at play here.

Someone wanted her and the evidence of the death camps erased simultaneously. But who?

She activated the rocket engines. The confined office space quickly filled with smoke. She lifted off the desk turned and flew directly at Virtue who was choking and disoriented. Her twin rockets slammed into his mid section causing him to emit a strangled grunt and the pistol flew from his hand. RED slammed him into a row of filing cabinets, which fell backward as if they were trees struck by hurricane force winds. Her sensors indicated his heart had a stopped upon impact with heavy steel cabinets. The office had been showered with his blood.

Knowing her pilot and close friend was dead she turned and flew to the door to the corridor. Once outside she used the sensors to find the opening to the exit. The walls and floor around her were trembling. Something very bad had happened.

Sure enough her sensors recorded a massive explosion somewhere to the north of her position centered within the facility. It occurred near the coordinates where Commander Heroic had been dropped off. The readings were heavy with deadly radiation of a type common to nuclear weapons.

RED increased the power to the rockets and her speed

increased until she shot out the exit at her maximum speed. She selected a course directly opposite of the direction of spreading wave of fiery all consuming energy and shot up and away into the night sky.

The pinpoint brilliant stars dotting the heavens were still visible against the darkness but the blast wave was edging out the peripheral edges of the visible sky as it grew like a pebble dropped in a pond more rapidly than RED would have liked.

RED added every bit of internal power to the thrusters and the speed edged slowly upward. The thrust increased beyond the design specifications. She was red lining the rocket motors. Every on board system was becoming compromised including her memory core.

Finally the motors began to shut down as they over heated and she began to tumble in the thin air. Gradually she became aware of her surroundings as her internal sensors recalibrated. She was higher in the atmosphere than she had ever been—more than 97,000 feet —and five hundred miles from where she started.

I'm gonna need a major refit.

She activated her thrusters and found her rockets were still operational having cooled enough after the wild ride she'd just taken. She started a slow spiral to reduce altitude. One the way down she thought about Virtues death and about who might be responsible for turning him against her. Who had enough influence to turn a loyal pilot against an AI and who might want her dead? She'd made any number of enemies over the years but most of them were either dead or in prison.

The League of Evil seemed an obvious suspect but they were a little too convenient. Besides destroying their own facility seemed a little drastic just to murder one AI and her pilot. But then what happened to LARP and Heroic?

She opened the ghost comm. "Team One to Team Two." Static. She tried again with the same result. Curious.

She next tried the civilian news broadcasts. After listening for several minutes she learned they were reporting a massive explosion inside LOE territory but nothing about casualties. More curious.

"RED to Admiral Roosevelt." She signaled again. This time there was a response, but on a very low frequency band. "This is a secure Imperial Security channel. Who is this?" said a curt female voice.

"This is Captain Virtue's AI, Reactive Energy Device." She used her full name not just her code name and she transmitted the security identification code the admiral had given her at their meeting.

Whoever was at the other end didn't respond for several seconds giving RED enough time to try a long-range sensor sweep to detect any sign of LARP and Heroic but she found nothing. Not even an echo of their signal remained. This was very odd.

"Who gave you this security code?" asked the security officer in an officious and aggressive tone.

"Admiral Roosevelt."

"We have no record of an Admiral Roosevelt...in fact we have no record of you."

It suddenly dawned on RED what must have happened. It had to be the only reasonable explanation. "What year is this?" she asked.

"What does that matter?" said the woman with obvious distain.

"Please. I need to know the year."

The woman snorted through a sudden burst of static. "It's 1943. Why? I'm getting some strange readings from you lady...are you really a reactive energy device?"

I somehow must have been transported fifteen years ahead in time. RED delinked the connection without responding. The conversation was headed for planet awkward questions and she didn't want to go there.

She needed to recruit a new pilot, fast. Anything could have happened by now. It was entirely possible she might be the only AI who survived what she had to assume was a purge to remove the pilots and the AI's. The League of Evil must be behind these events.

She was not only going to fight on to rescue the empire from grip of the LOE but she would have to find a new and improved version of Captain Virtue to take the fight to whoever was responsible. Together they would be the heroes for this new age. The road ahead would be filled with danger and adventure and she was going to enjoy it.

Captain Virtue and RED will return in Captain Virtue Flies Again.

ABOUT THE AUTHOR

International selling Star Trek author, Russ Crossley under the name R.G. Hart, wrote a number of successful romances but now exclusively writes science fiction and fantasy, and mystery/suspense as well as their various subgenres. His latest science fiction short novels involve the mercenary team, Blaster Squad. Set in the far future this fast paced, action adventure series is available in print, ebook, and now books 1, 2, and 3 are available as audio books. The 7th and final book in the current story line will be available soon. He has sold several short stories that have appeared in anthologies from various publishers including; WMG Publishing, Pocket Books, 53rd Street Publishing, and St. Martins Press. He is past president of the Greater Vancouver Chapter of Romance Writers of America. He is also an alumni of the Oregon Coast Professional Fiction Writers Master Class taught by award winning author/editors, Kristine Katherine Rusch and Dean Wesley Smith. Feel free to contact him on Facebook, Twitter, or his website http//:www.russcrossley.com. He loves to hear from readers.

WAR EAGLE

Rita Schulz

Ruby Eagle, known to her close friends as Ruby Flare, was an international hero, a diminutive but fierce hummingbird. She stretched out her hand, just this once, to gently touch the orange-and-yellow sleek, tight-fitting uniform she used to wear.

She loved the way the red sparkly accent fabric at the throat shimmered in the light. It looked full of life. Ready to go. She ran her hand over the smooth, hard metal surface of her rocket pack with its green leather harness and wondered if she would ever use it to fly again.

She eyed the smaller uniform next to hers. It was green and blue, with the same deep red throat. Her greatest wish was that her daughter Anna would take her place as a Hummingbird, an elite division of the Atlantean War Eagles, but Anna was completely against the idea. She didn't want to even hear the old stories and legends of the great Atlanteans and their history.

Ruby closed the shatterproof, sparkling clean glass case, turned, and slowly limped away, trying not to lean on her smooth red arbutus cane as she stepped back.

It had been a long time since she had been in her secret space. Her large, hidden workroom contained her uniforms, weapons, and computers. It was an area about twelve feet by eighteen feet, a good-sized room specifically designed to have it's own private entrance besides the one in her closet—two of them in fact, one from a balcony and the other from her private elevator. Outside her workroom in the penthouse, there wasn't a trace of the entry. In fact, there was no indication a hidden room existed.

She stepped into her closet and pushed the wooden panel that closed the doorway to her hidden workroom.

The closet, with all its clothes, different textures, and colors, shifted and drifted around her as she walked through it into her bedroom. The smell of roses and lavender softly enveloped her as she walked.

The morning news echoed from the radio next to her bed. The world was in turmoil. It needed true leadership and heroes more than ever. She held back the tears filling her eyes and threatening to spill down her cheeks. She held back the grief as she chose the clothes she would wear today. An aqua long sleeved shirt with comfortable black leggings seemed to fit her mood.

The aqua looked wonderful with her dark blonde hair and green eyes, and the leggings suited her petite, slender figure.

She went to her nightstand and checked her cell phone. Good. No calls. It had been quiet over the last week. Just the way she liked it. No news was good news.

She looked in her full-length mirror and debated whether to tie back her shoulder-length hair as the apartment doorbell rang, interrupting her thoughts. Then she heard a key turn in the lock. Ruby knew it must be her daughter Anna. Anna always rang first to let her knew someone was there so she wouldn't be startled, then used her key to enter the apartment.

She looked at the time. What had happened? Somehow she had lost an hour. That can't be correct. There was no way she had been staring at the uniform, dreaming her life away for an hour. It was a life she had never wanted.

"Mom, Mom! Are you here?" called her daughter as she entered the spacious apartment. The large picture windows facing the sun-washed False Creek provided breathtaking views and plenty of light, bathing the room in a glow. There was every kind of vessel in the harbor, from small people ferries to magnificent yachts moving as if in a chaotic ballet.

"I'm in the bedroom, Anna," Ruby called as she put her super power of speed to the test and was dressed in less than three seconds. She smiled when she walked out of the bedroom, smoothing her hair as she hurried to the hallway.

"Are you okay, Mom? You look kind of flushed. And you didn't answer your cell when I called earlier," asked Anna as she tipped her head to one side causing her shoulder-length dark blonde hair to fall over one shoulder. She studied her mother carefully, her brow wrinkled.

"Oh, I'm fine. Everything is good. Time just got away from me. Where do you want to go for lunch?" Ruby said as she opened the hall coat closet and pulled out a light blue rain jacket, which she slipped on, then pulled out her gray leather cross-body purse and slipped it over her head, draping it comfortably across her body. She glanced at her cane and her lips formed a thin line. She hated the stupid thing but knew if she didn't take it, Anna would comment on it. Or worse, pick it up and hand it to her.

Why did Anna insist on giving her such a hard time? She was doing everything that the stupid physiotherapist told her to do, but the strength to her right leg still wasn't coming back and her balance was off, too. After a year and a half, she felt like she would never be able to walk properly again, never mind fly, land and fight smoothly with her rocket pack. She was a superhero who was grounded and her power of super speed was only good for getting dressed in a hurry. What a stupid waste.

"Anna, I was thinking I would stay home from the council

meeting in Berlin this year. I've been to every meeting over the last twenty-eight years. That's six times in a row, not counting all the special meetings. We have other approved members who can go in my place." She checked her jacket pockets for her keys. They weren't there.

She shook her body bag and heard the jangling sound and smiled. She really should get one of the clickers that are so popular with her friends, but she thought those things were stupid. It was as if her friends were getting old and couldn't remember anything. At forty-seven years of age, she certainly wasn't old and neither were her friends. They were just lazy and couldn't be bothered to try remembering. They didn't exercise their minds at all.

Anna's eyebrows furrowed as she looked at her mother with concern all over her narrow features.

"Look, Mom, we don't have to go out for lunch if you don't want to. You need time to figure this all out."

"What are you talking about, Anna?"

Anna paused before she answered her mother. Her expression shifted between shocked and confused.

"Mom, our representation for the Atlanteans in the leading five hundred families is hanging on by a thread," said Anna as she went into the kitchen and poured herself a glass of cool tea from a jug in the fridge.

"Anna, I don't know what you're talking about. We are well represented this year, only missing a few people. The Grays are in Africa on a working holiday."

"What? You do know that four of our members have recently died and three are on holidays. Yes, the Grays are serving in Africa with the Doctors Without Borders; that only leaves one more qualified representative. If something happens to them, well.... You have to go," said Anna, her tone firm.

"I haven't heard anything about members dying," said Ruby. "They would have called me. I'm the family's first contact person. Everything like that would go through me."

"Mom, I've been calling you. A couple of times this morning, too, and you haven't been answering. The messages go right to voice mail, and the last time I tried to leave you a message, your answering service said your mailbox was full. What's going on?" said Anna as she crossed her arms over her chest. She finished her tea and set the glass in the sink.

Ruby nodded at her daughter, watching her eyes carefully. Was Anna trying to play a trick on her? She looked at her cell phone, tapped her code into it, and slowly put the phone to her ear. There were twenty-two missed calls and ten of them were marked urgent. Something was very wrong with her phone.

"Oh dear. I see what you mean. Just give me a minute to check my messages." Ruby ambled into the large second bedroom that doubled as a guest bedroom and her office.

The walls were painted light gray with a soft blue-gray feature wall. The room was comfortable and relaxing. Two of the walls were lined in warm oak bookshelves full of books. Another wall had an oak roll-top desk and two chairs on the sides of the desk, one a stationary chair and the other a rolling leather office chair.

She pulled up the top of the roll-top, laid her phone on the desktop, then pulled the office chair in place and picked up a pen and pad of paper lying on the desktop.

Ruby quickly took notes as she went through the messages. Some she deleted and others she forwarded to her computer and special files.

Anna stood silently in the doorway, watching. Finally she said, "Mom, is there something I can do to help?"

Ruby glanced up and shook her head until she once more focused on her messages and notes.

Ruby's secret desire was that Anna would take up her position in the War Eagle Council and on the council of the Five Hundred Families. Anna's position was one of inheritance through Ruby, and before that, her grandmother. But until now Anna had refused anything to do with her inheritance, including her gifts as an Atlantean.

Anna had inherited the natural quick agility, speed, and balance that was far superior to average humans and something she always hid when among normal humans. Even Ruby didn't know the true extent of Anna's gifts since they differed greatly from person to person.

Ruby held her desire for her daughter close to her heart and very seldom mentioned it around her. Ruby knew the more she pushed, the more Anna would do the opposite.

Ruby also knew for Anna to commit to the council and take her place as royalty in the War Eagle clan, and more importantly the Meeting of the Five Hundred, Anna would need to do so without any coaxing from her mother.

These life-changing decisions were something Ruby's mother had left for her to decide as well. Her mother told that if she took on the position, her life would change immediately and forever. There was no going back, no change of mind later, no abdicating. It was big stuff.

Ruby realized that she did not have the time she needed to find out all the details of what had been happening with the family. She would have to prioritize to take care of the largest concerns.

She checked the dates on her messages and realized she had been out of touch for twenty-four hours. How had that happened?

She remembered going out for dinner with her sister Marana the night before—they had never been close, but got along fine. They had gone for Japanese food, one of her favorites, at a local place she had eaten at regularly for years.

"Mom, are you okay?" asked Anna.

"Yes, I'm fine." Ruby changed the subject. "I was just thinking about what happened last night."

"Well, what happened?"

"Nothing much. Marana came over and we went out for dinner at Sushi's on Main. I had a bento box and brought half of it home.

The only thing different from my usual dinner was that we had some saké."

"You had a drink? That's fine, not something you do all the time, but every once in a while," said Anna. She disappeared back into the kitchen and Ruby heard the sounds associated with her daughter making tea.

"Yes, I know," Ruby called after her, "but the strange thing was that Marana ordered it and when it came, she poured it for me but she didn't have any herself. She filled my little porcelain cup a few times, but not hers."

Anna walked back into the office. She shrugged. "Maybe she decided she didn't feel like it. You know she's flighty. I'm surprised you had dinner with her actually. A family dinner I understand, but not a private dinner. How is Shannon, my dear cousin?" Anna went back into the kitchen to get fresh tea bags out of the cupboard. Ruby followed her.

"I know you've never gotten along with Shannon."

"I got along with her just fine until I realized Shannon couldn't be trusted and neither could Aunt Marana. They really are an interesting line of the family. Our family is considered royalty and don't care or really want the family and international obligation, and they really, really want it." Anna poured hot water into the teapot to warm it.

"Yes, you're right. We have the obligation and they don't, so that's why the job looks so glamorous to them and they covet it. It must seem like no work and only fun for us." Ruby sat down at the round blond maple kitchen table.

Ruby ran her fingertips over the smooth, light-colored, warm wood. She loved the feel of it. It was as if it were alive and was one of the few pieces she still had from Atlantis.

Anna brought the tea and mugs to the table. They both took their tea black so it was very simple.

"Thank you, Anna," Ruby said as Anna poured the tea. Ruby put her hands around the warm mug to comfort herself.

"Mom," Anna began, her eyes serious. "There's something we need to discuss." After a short pause she continued. "It's something I didn't think I would ever talk to you about." Anna picked up her teacup and took a sip.

Ruby took a small sip of her tea as she calmed and centered herself. She was determined she would not show any emotion, good or bad, at what Anna was about to tell her. All she could do was hope. She waited.

"I spoke with Shannon—actually, she spoke with me—she wants to take your place on the council. Before you freak, let me finish," said Anna, looking into her mother's eyes pleadingly.

Ruby looked at the tabletop as she lifted her hands up and steepled them. She took in slow, deep breaths. Rage started to build in her belly. How dare Shannon contact Anna and tell her daughter she wanted Ruby's position on the council. The girl was a greedy airhead and it always seemed all she wanted to do was party.

Ruby slowly locked eyes with her daughter.

"What are you saying, Anna?" Her tone sounded menacing even to her.

Anna appeared unfazed. "I think I need to go with you to the council meeting this year and find out about who I am, as an Atlantean, and what your position entails. I need to find out exactly what I'm thinking of turning down before my dear cousin Shannon tries to take it. When do we leave?" asked Anna, smiling faintly at her mother.

Ruby recognized a faint glimmer of fear in Anna's eyes and she nodded to reassure her daughter.

A few weeks later, Ruby packed her things and asked Anna to back up her computer and email and pack those to take with them too. They would stop off at Anna's modest apartment to pick up her things and then they would be off.

"Mom, can I drive the car? Please? You've been saying maybe for a very long time and you're with me right now," pleaded Anna as they took Ruby's apartment elevator to the parking garage where her vintage red mustang convertible was parked. With a grin, Anna grabbed the car keys from her mother's hand and dropped the keys into her own light green jacket.

They'd take it to the airport.

Ruby shook her head as she watched the young girl who along the way had changed from her daughter into a talented young woman.

Anna was now a successful fiction writer, just like her mother. It had been a long time since Ruby had realized Anna was an adult— since her twenty-fifth birthday, and that had been three years ago.

Ruby took a deep breath and nodded. Unable to contain her excitement, Anna whooped with joy and gave her mother a quick hug as she swung the driver's door open after putting their suitcases in the trunk.

They both slipped into the car's tan leather seats, gently hugged by the luxurious interior.

"Now remember, this is a very special car," cautioned Ruby. A long time ago she'd had the car modified so it was one of the fastest cars on the road—and one of the only things she had left from her husband, who had died ten years ago in an accident when his rocket pack stalled during high aerial practice.

"I know, Mom," said Anna, then gave the candy apple red, black-roofed convertible a little more gas than was needed, causing the powerful car to lurch slightly. She laughed as she braked to a stop, shifted into reverse, then back into drive and drove out of the garage onto the street.

It was a beautiful, warm, sunny day in Vancouver. The sky was blue with a few high white clouds—a perfect summer day.

They arrived at the airport in less than half an hour and Anna smiled warmly at the long-term parking attendant. Once they were parked, they took out their suitcases and flagged down the shuttle to take them to the international terminal for their flight to Berlin.

Ruby gazed at Anna. Her eyes were sparkling and her cheeks glowed. Her daughter was obviously excited. She had been to Berlin before as a visitor, but Ruby knew this was going to be a different kind of trip for her. Something special.

They would be in Berlin for two weeks and Anna would have to listen and learn a lot of new things she had purposefully not wanted to learn before.

Nine hours later they arrived in Berlin after a very comfortable trip. Anna loved being in business class—her first time—Ruby had splurged on them both.

Ruby wondered if her sisters, nieces and nephews, and cousins would show up at the meeting or just use this as a trip to go shopping or traveling, which was their usual excuse for their summer holiday.

The excitement and apprehension grew like a peach pit in Ruby's belly. Anna was facing a massive learning curve and a decision that would mean her life would change forever. Would both their lives change? Of course her life would change was she ready to do that? Not be the leader? What would happen if and when Ruby's standing in the family changed and a new leader was chosen? How would she feel? What would she do especially if she couldn't be a Hummingbird warrior?

Ruby sat next to Anna at the baggage carousel, waiting for their luggage to come down. She struggled to remain calm, but her heart was beating fast. She hoped she had packed everything they would need, but only time would tell.

Ruby went over and over the information she would have to cover with Anna in her mind. Should she deal with the history of their family first or their abilities? Anna never had liked history growing up. It was one of her worst subjects at school. Ruby kept reminding herself Anna was an adult. Maybe she should just let Anna ask questions on topics, answer them, and make sure that everything was covered.

"Mom, look who's here." Anna said brightly. "It's Shannon and Aunt Marana; why do you think they're here?"

Ruby looked around the busy arrivals area trying to locate their chauffeur.

"Anna! Anna, how are you?" said Shannon as she smiled at Anna and moved in for an air kiss. She stepped back and arched a disapproving eyebrow at Ruby. "Hello, Aunt Ruby, I see you've both come to Berlin. What are you doing here?" Shannon asked Ruby with a strange glint in her eyes.

Anan spoke first, her lips forming a tight line. "We're here for the meeting, at least Mom is. What are you doing here? Shopping?" She stole a glance at her mother, who gave a slight shake of her head.

"How are you, Shannon?" asked Ruby, her attention on their surroundings, trying to spot their chauffer among the crowd of passengers.

"I guess you haven't heard," said Shannon with a smirk on her lips. "You were too busy, I assume? There's an open spot for another representative on the council since the Amazons are no longer a voting group."

The Atlanteans and the Amazons usually voted together as the Peace Delegation and sought to bring better solutions to the table of the Five Hundred.

Ruby's heart hammered hard. If this was true, there would be trouble—and she hadn't heard back from one of their own representatives. She would have to make sure that they had their own quorum at the next meeting.

Ruby caught Anna's attention with a nod. "Stay here with our luggage and keep your eyes open for the driver," Ruby said. She spoke low so only Anna would hear over the crowd noise, then shifted her attention to her niece.

"Yes, Shannon. Thank you for letting us know the news. Have a nice holiday and say hello to your mother. Are you staying at the

Royal Gardens?"

Shannon nodded, offering Ruby an insincere smile.

Before she left them, Ruby noticed the pulse on Shannon's throat and realized she was extremely excited and struggling to hide her feelings.

"Yes, we'll be there. See you soon," said Shannon with a pout on her lips as she glared at them before she turned and walked away toward her mother.

"You're doing very well," Ruby assured her daughter. "We'll talk more when we get into our hotel rooms." The crowds began to dissipate and Ruby grinned when she saw their chauffer holding a placard with their names on it not far from the exit doors.

The chauffer came over with two baggage carts and started to load their luggage. Ruby saw the man's grim expression as he handled two of their suitcases that she knew were heavy. After all, she had packed them.

Once at the hotel, Ruby and Anna entered their reserved two-bedroom suite. Ruby watched Anna's joyful expression out of the corner of one eye as Anna looked around the double king-size rooms they would be sharing.

It was a large space done in cream and taupe with touches of gold and red; there was a soft scent of roses and lavender in the air. It was a very sumptuous room with two long couches set across from each other, a coffee table in a high gloss mahogany that matched the end tables, and a large dining room table with seating for eight. There was a spectacular crystal chandelier hanging over the table that caught the light, spraying it over the walls and ceiling like glitter.

Anna looked at her mother and grinned as the bellhop opened the two oak doors with etched glass that led to the bedrooms. She stood in awe, gazing upon what would be her room for the duration.

"If you could put those cases into my room it would be very helpful," Anna said to the bellhop as she took hold of the cart she wanted and started to push it into the room on the right side of the suite.

"Thank you, Anna," Ruby said. "I'm sure that...Bernard, yes?" The bellhop nodded. "Can do that for us. Now he knows where we'd like our individual cases."

In a few moments their luggage was stored in the correct rooms and Anna was picking at the fruit basket on the dining room table.

"I see you're hungry," said Ruby gently as she handed the bellhop a generous tip before he closed the main door after himself and left them alone.

Ruby pulled out her cell phone and her laptop and set herself up at the large wooden desk next to the ornate fireplace. Soon she had everything up and running, with her yellow legal pad ready with sticky pads, pens, and pencils.

"First, I need to check on the other representatives for us and make sure they are here or on their way. Then I'll get hold of the Amazon contingent and find out what happened with them and figure our how to rectify it. We need both of our groups to act and vote as the Peace Hummingbirds," said Ruby.

Anna looked at her mother and smiled, her eyes filling with pride as she saw her mother in her take-charge mode.

"I'm sorry about this, Anna. I guess we'll be discussing things and you'll have to learn very quickly. We work on Roberts Rules. Here's my copy." Ruby held up a small, dingy-gray, dog-eared booklet and tossed Anna a bright white one, "and here is a copy for you. You will need to memorize sections of it."

The house phone started to ring at the same time Ruby's cell phone started vibrating. Anna picked up the house phone and started talking on it. Ruby picked up her cell as she slid Anna a legal pad on the dining room table and a couple of pens. Notes, she mouthed.

Anna was glowing, her eyes were bright, and she was taking notes as if she had been doing this her entire life. Ruby was proud of her and very, very glad she had come on this trip. Ruby had a feeling this was going to be the hardest conference she had ever attended.

"Mom, I just got a message from the Gray's," said Anna as she quickly wrote down a note on her legal pad.

"Good, I called them before we left home to ask them to come to Berlin in case we need another alternate."

"Yes, but the message is that they can't make it. There's been an Ebola outbreak in Africa and they can't get their exit visas approved," Anna turned to face her mother.

"But, Mom, that's not the important thing. They tried to get hold of you today and couldn't get through to your phone. They got us on the hotel phone. I don't understand why you're not...just a minute." Anna picked up her cell and dialed Ruby's number. She watched her mother and the cell phone in her mother's right hand intently.

Nothing happened.

"I'm not getting anything, not even a message prompt. Something has happened to your phone. And I think—"

"It started when I went out for dinner with Marana," Ruby interrupted, pursing her lips.

Anna tapped the end button. "Yes, dear Aunt Marana and Shannon are in it together," she growled. "I think they're making a bid for your seat...our seat. We have to stop them. There seems a lot more to these events."

There was a knock on the door, startling them both. Anna got up from the table and went to answer it.

She opened the door to discover a tall man dressed all in black, with a knee-length cape over his black pants and dress shirt. "Is Ruby Eagle, the leader of the house of Atlantis, here? I have a message for her."

Ruby got up, stood tall, and gracefully walked to the door. "I am Ruby Eagle from the house of Atlantis. How can I help you?"

He pulled out a black, heavy, long glove and slapped Ruby's left cheek with it, startling her. "I am here to present you with a request to meet this afternoon in the meadow behind the hotel for a duel with Shannon Brown for the position of representative of the Atlantis War Eagles. Do you accept the challenge?"

Ruby looked confused, dazed. What was happening? Her family had held this seat for the last five generations. They'd never dueled over it.

Anna strode past her mother to approach the messenger. Once there, she snatched the glove from his hand and slapped him hard across his left cheek, leaving a red mark.

"You may tell Shannon Brown that Anna Eagle accepts the challenge and will be stepping in as Ruby Eagle's champion," Anna said in an assertive manner. She shifted her gaze to Ruby. "Correct, Mother?"

"Anna....I can't let you. It's too dangerous," stammered Ruby as thoughts and memories of her late husband Galvin's death and her own near fatal accident flashed through her mind.

"Mom, trust me. I know what I'm doing."

Ruby nodded, her eyes still not focusing due to the unexpected blow across her face, but she knew she needed to trust her daughter.

"Yes, Anna Eagle is my champion," said Ruby with a resigned tone in her voice.

The messenger nodded, and with a swirl of his black cloak, he was gone to deliver their reply.

"Anna, what are you doing? You can't—"

"Mom, I understand you want to protect me and keep me safe," interjected Anna with a calm but stern voice.

"Don't you talk to me in that tone of voice."

"Mom, come with me." Anna led Ruby toward her bedroom. "I don't want to fight with you, but there are things you need to know." Anna opened her bedroom door and walked to her suitcases. She hadn't had time to put her things away. Ruby walked stiffly from the doorway.

Anna tossed one of her cases on the bed, opened it, and pulled out her hummingbird costume, which she laid on the bed. Then she opened another heavy case and pulled out her rocket pack and put it next to her costume.

"Mom, you don't know this, but I know all about the costumes and the rocket packs."

Ruby stood there, her eyes wide as she nervously licked her lips.

"No, you don't...it can't be..." A knot of tension tightened her stomach. "How did you get that out of my secret workroom?"

"Mom, I've known about your workroom for years—since I was in university. Right after you gave me a house key, I'd wait until you were out and I'd come over to your place and check it out thoroughly."

"But....you can't know. I've been waiting to explain everything to you." Ruby looked at Anna through watery eyes.

"How did you know how to accept a challenge and declare a champion? Where did that idea come from?"

A whisper of a grin passed over Anna's narrow features. "I know you wanted to teach me, and I want you to, but I first went to Grandma and asked her. That's why I spent so much time with her in the last years of her life; that, and I really loved her."

Ruby looked at Anna as if she was seeing her daughter for the first time.

There was a sharp knock on the door. They stared at it, neither of them moving.

Ruby watched Anna disappear in a blur of super speed to the door, pause, then open it. "Anna Eagle, you have been summoned. What say you?"

"I answer and come with you," said Anna as she went into her bedroom and, in a flash, came out dressed in her costume and rocket pack. "Let's go," she said.

"Ruby Eagle?" said the man in the cape. "You have been summoned." He handed Ruby a manila envelope. "This summons is for you and explains why you have been stripped of your seat."

The messenger turned back to Anna, nodded, and they both went down the hall.

Ruby scanned the documents from the envelope as the man left. It said that she was in violation of her position of leader of the remaining Atlanteans. It cited that she was out of contact with her people and had abandoned her position as their leader.

Ruby was so upset that she was shaking. How dare they? She knew that dear Marana and Shannon had something to do with this. Now "all" she had to do was save Anna, an untrained War Eagle, from battling her cousin, and restore her representative seat with the War Eagles in time for the conference of the Five Hundred.

With Anna gone, Ruby decided she, too, needed to adopt her superhero persona. Her costume and rocket pack were also in her luggage.

Ruby was soon changed and headed to the meadow behind the hotel. She decided to fly; it had been a long time since she had used her rocket pack and it would be marvelous to be flying again.

She discovered there were at least fifty people waiting at the meadow when she arrived overhead but there was no sign of Anna or Shannon. She wondered how they had all found out about the duel. Normally a duel was a quiet, dignified affair and only had the challenger and the responder, with their seconds, in attendance. But this was like a media show. She even noticed cameras, and people also were using their cell phones to record the event. This was going to go viral on the Internet.

Ruby realized that she had forgotten to ask Anna who had trained her in aerial combat. She had mentioned that her grandmother had told her the history, but who had actually made sure she knew how to work the rocket pack?

As Ruby landed a short distance from the field, she heard a loud shout from the people gathered there. She looked over and saw Anna striding toward the meeting area. She had to hurry—Anna didn't have a second. Then she saw Marana come and stand beside Anna.

Ruby's heart hammered. She had trusted Marana at dinner and with the saké. It seemed that Anna had trusted her aunt as well. What fools they both were.

Ruby watched Anna turn on her rocket pack and it sent her up at a tilted angle to the meadow. When she came down, it was at a steep, sideways angle. She could see the jets on the rocket pack sputter and almost misfire. What was she doing? Then Ruby watched Marana and Shannon start to laugh and realized she and Anna had been completely set up. Anna could die. This wasn't a game. People had died during duels in the past, which is why they were rare these days.

She had to get to her only child. She had to take over for her champion. Ruby was still the Atlantean leader. She had never read anything that said she couldn't take over for her champion at a duel.

She watched as Shannon gracefully rose in the azure sky. Her costume was crimson red and purple, something Ruby had never seen before. Shannon did a few passes around Anna and smiled at Anna's awkward, jerky movements with the rocket pack.

As if a lightbulb had been suddenly turned on, the information fell into place for Ruby. Shannon and Marana were in this together and had sabotaged her communications network. It looked like they had done the same to Anna's training and rocket pack. How could they? They were supposed to be family.

Then she knew her sister's actions were all in the name of jealousy, that evil green-eyed monster. They were willing to kill Anna for their own advancement. Perhaps there was even more at stake with the control of the Five Hundred and the global economy.

Ruby didn't have any more time. Instinctively her fingers found the settings she needed on the rocket pack controls and soon she was flying toward the meadow at top speed. Normally these duels were conducted at a high altitude and out in the countryside so no spectators would be hurt. This place wasn't ideal, but her sister and niece had given her little choice.

Ruby landed next to Anna and looked at her daughter. She hated to do this and hoped Anna wouldn't be embarrassed, but it was her life she was trying to protect.

"Anna, thank you for standing in for me and the War Eagles, but I think I can take it from here. Maybe you can help me with another problem, okay?" She saw a look of concern cross Anna's face.

"Certainly, Mom, if you feel up to it. I relinquish the challenge to you," Anna said calmly before she turned off her rocket pack.

"No problem, Anna. While I take care of this, why don't you get the Speaker and the Parliamentarian as witnesses to this challenge? That way they can make a record of it."

Anna's shoulders visibly relaxed. She smiled at her mother before pulling out her cell phone to make the call.

"Shannon, I answer your challenge and take over for my Champion. Shall we begin in ten minutes?" asked Ruby as she floated again in the air close to Shannon and Marana, then gently set herself on the soft grass near them.

Shannon was having a heated discussion with Marana and Marana was getting angry.

"You can't do that!" yelled Shannon, her eyes blazing with fury. "I challenged Anna, not you. Anna stepped in as your Champion."

Ruby could now see what had happened. Marana had convinced Shannon that she would go up against someone who had no idea how to operate a rocket pack, never mind fight with one. But Shannon and Marana knew that Ruby was very good with a rocket pack and was an excellent fighter.

"Shannon, you actually challenged the leader of the Atlanteans, and that would be me. Anna was my Champion, but I am going to fight myself, so the Challenge is mine. Come on now, are we going to fight or are you going to forfeit the challenge—forever?"

Ruby spoke with an amplified, booming voice and smiled as she saw the Speaker and Parliamentarian had arrived, standing on the rise overlooking the vast meadow, watching.

Ruby shifted her gaze back at Shannon in time to see Marana

deliver an open-handed slap across her daughter's face. Ruby stopped herself from interfering with the mother and daughter, at least for now.

Ruby saw Shannon turn off her rocket pack and turn to face her, eyes focused on her feet. "I concede the challenge. You are the leader of the Atlanteans by heredity and valor."

Ruby nodded and looked at the Speaker. "Have you witnessed?"

He answered, "We have. The challenge has been met and will be recorded."

Ruby nodded as Anna flew to her and landed at her side.

"Grandmother always said 'if you need to fight or go to war rather than peaceful discussion, you have already lost.' Today we solved our differences peacefully."

Ruby smiled at her daughter. "Your grandmother was correct. The forces of war have been stopped. For now."

ABOUT THE AUTHOR

Rita lives on the Sunshine Coast in British Columbia with, Russ, her husband, who is also a fiction writer. She has written for many years and is an alumnus of the Oregon Writers Network Master class, and the Greater Vancouver Chapter of the Romance Writers of America. Her most recently published novels include the western romance, *Fire in Their Hearts* with Russ Crossley, the mystery *Old Bones*, and the collection of pirate fiction, *Ladies of the Jolly Roger* all published by 53rd Street Publishing.

Please visit her website at http://www.ritaschulz.com to view her other works.

EFFICIENT ENGINEERING

Mary Jo Rabe

Michelle's puffy blue eyes watered. The habitat air cleaners no longer did an adequate job of removing the caustic Martian dust from inside the dome. If her watery eyes weren't enough proof, then the quivering in her nose from the slight scent of peroxide should be. Damn. Even the chocolate pudding in the cafeteria was starting to taste like bleach. She was getting so tired of this dust.

Her workshop was three stories beneath ground level, which reduced the noise from machinery, boisterous colony celebrations, and Martian weather, but didn't keep the damned surface dust from descending, silently, stealthily, steadily. And if the dust got down this far, it was probably more noticeable closer to the surface. Damn.

She needed to return a few air scrubber spare parts after all. Fortunately everything was in its properly organized place in the storeroom. And the situation was temporary. If things continued as planned, she wouldn't have to spend the rest of her life in this bureaucratic paradise. She hadn't given up her dreams of exploring just to vegetate in a safe and boring environment, even on a planet other than the one she had been born on.

Some people appreciated the quadruple backups and redundancy, claiming it made the Martian colony safe, even if equipment didn't always run efficiently. Michelle had hoped to leave such obsessive people behind on Earth. But they always seemed to follow her, to college, to post-doc fellowships, to Mars.

When she applied for this job, she pictured the Mars outpost as being a stepping stone to the rest of the universe where adventurers would lead the way, her dream come true. Instead pencil pushers and bean counters invented new rules almost daily. Success was if no one died or was injured, even if that meant the entire colony just huddled timidly underground. Not what she signed up for, not what she dreamed about ever since she entranced by the first starry, starry night back in Iowa.

Her spacious elevator — something she had gotten into the original design of the settlement along with the extra warehouse, i.e. storeroom — screeched plaintively. That was a problem she had to put at the top of her list. This elevator had to function perfectly when the time came for it to transport certain pieces of a heavy load to the surface.

As colony habitat mechanic, repair person, and engineer on call for everyone and everything, Michelle of course had universal access to processes and equipment. For her official settlement activities she kept scrupulously honest books. For various personal requests involving bending a significant number of rules she demanded and generally got a certain degree of discretion from her customers.

The door to her workshop beeped and Michelle quickly assessed her appearance in the shiny door to the storeroom. She was no longer young and foolish, but also not yet old and acquiescent. Her baggy, blue jumpsuit hid her well-toned muscles just as the lacy pink gloves hid the inevitable bruises on her hands from free-lance mechanical activity. Her blonde hair was a few millimeters shorter than the week before, but definitely not enough to be noticed, though now barely covering the tops of her ears. All she had to do before greeting whoever wanted something from her was to contort her perhaps larcenous facial expressions into a look of stern but benevolent helpfulness.

The door slid open and Roger, the current colony teenage heart-throb, swaggered in. His lean and lanky physique was clad attractively in expensive jogging attire with its fake strategically-placed patches. His artistically designed mound of red hair (Was it supposed to represent Olympus Mons this week?) added the desired centimeters to his height and distracted somewhat from the oafish expression on his face.

"Yo, Dr. Michelle," he began, leaning over her touch-sensitive monitor table.

Michelle smiled slightly more broadly than she at first intended. This was an extremely welcome visitor.

"Yo, Roger," she answered, waving her hand in acknowledgment or whatever the current mode of greetings for the not-ready-for-adult-responsibilities generation was.

"What can I help you with today?"

Roger strained his facial muscles, trying to turn his cagey smile into a charming one. Michelle noted that he still needed practice with this maneuver.

"Could you, uh, look at our rocket transporters?" he asked. "There's something wrong with the speed regulators."

Michelle stared at him. "And what exactly is wrong?" she asked. "The materials transporters are all standard construction and allow speeds necessary for planetary transport activity." While rattling off the usual phrases, she did the mental calculations.

"No, no," Roger said. "Not true, maybe in factory specifications, but not in real life. A lot of us pilots have gotten in dangerous situations because we couldn't achieve necessary speed fast enough."

"For your illegal rocket drag races," Michelle thought. Adolescent males and their need for speed, one of the constants of this universe.

She sighed somewhat theatrically and walked toward the elevator. "Well, then, let's go and take a look," she said.

"What?" Roger said, obviously expecting to have to plead longer.

"Take me to the rocket station and we'll unlock your ships so I can check all the pertinent parts," Michelle said patiently. "Maybe there is something I can adjust."

Returning, accompanied by a robot container transporter she had programmed to be amiable, Michelle mentally assessed her haul of useful assorted spare parts. Current Mars colony regulations demanded a quadruple redundancy in every area. Michelle had left the transporter rockets with a triple redundancy, more than adequate for most foreseeable situations. Since she also removed the automatic speed inhibitors, created specifically to prevent rocket racing, the youthful pilots were unlikely to report her helpful manipulations. Success.

She of course logged the legal and required inspection of the rocket station and transport rockets. The programming and hacking techniques she had learned in college turned out to be one of her most useful skills here on Mars. For her endeavors in the near future though, her creative manipulation of nanobots was more important. Those little critters had to keep her alive and kicking for a long, long time. She needed this time for the exploring she dreamed of doing.

Her communicator was flashing all kinds of colored lights. Checking her calendar, Michelle chose to call Betty, the cafeteria lady, first.

"Thank you" Betty's lined face framed by long, curly, white hair rose up from the table in a hologram. "Do you have a moment? You probably can't help me, but I need to vent. That idiot settlement manager ..."

"What now?" Michelle interrupted.

"He insists that we follow the Earth rules to the letter. I'm supposed to store all foodstuffs in four times the amount we need. You know I don't have the space to store all this. I hate wasting the time preserving all the food when the fields and gardens function so well now that we can provide fresh vegetables and will never use the aging supplies."

"So dump them," Michelle said.

"You know I can't. The rules demand ..."

Michelle nodded. The time was right. "Eventually they'll have to change the rules for the cafeteria," she said. "In the meantime I can transfer some of your supplies to one of my storerooms. That will give you a little more flexibility."

"Thank you," Betty said. "That would be a great help! When can you empty out some of my shelves?"

"Right now," Michelle answered. "I assume I can rely on your, shall we say, discretion about moving these supplies."

"Damn right," Betty yelled, and Michelle reprogrammed her transporter robot to pick up the food and had some warehouse robots make room for them.

The workshop door beeped again, and Michelle exited her secret storeroom at the back of the workshop, sliding the concealment wall behind her. The settlement's assistant director, a tall, skinny, middle-aged man with greedy eyes and thinning hair, walked into her workshop and sat down on her chair without asking. Michelle was still lost in thought from her activity in the storeroom and therefore didn't notice his smirk immediately.

"Mr. Himmelsbeck," she asked. "Can I help you?"

"I'm sure we can come to an understanding," he answered, moving his scrawny hands over her touch-sensitive monitor table, making holograms jump up and down.

Pointing to her communicator, Michelle said, "As you can see, I have more than enough emergencies to attend to."

"You're a brazen thief," he replied.

"No, I'm the overworked engineer who keeps this settlement functional while you bureaucrats dream up new rules to make life on Mars unbearable," Michelle said calmly. "If you're just here to call me names, record your message and I'll get back to you."

Himmelsbeck slapped her monitor table and a hologram document rose a meter above the surface. "It's all there," he said, moving his bony index finger down the list. "Spare parts, supplies, food, nanobots, medical equipment and ingredients, all missing after the colony engineer made unnecessary repairs, endangering the safety of the entire colony."

"No one who requested repairs considered them unnecessary," Michelle said. "Redundant safety features often sacrifice efficiency, and sometimes efficiency is more important to people who have work to do. All the work I do here is meticulously documented." Apparently she must have forgotten to delete some files over time. Well, she was getting impatient to leave.

"Certainly," Mr. Himmelsbeck agreed. "Your official repair work is documented but not the illegal favors you do for individual colony members. You've been squirreling away equipment ever since you got here."

"Nope," Michelle said as she scrolled through the messages on her communicator. "And the burden of proof is on you." Naturally her secret warehouse/storeroom was no longer documented in any of the construction plans and she thought she had adjusted the permanent digital records every time she moved equipment from one place to another.

"You made a sentimental mistake," he said, smiling. "You added features to the toys in the pre-school, features for which there were no spare parts on the inventory lists. That made me wonder, and then I started searching. Every now and then I found something. With enough time, and I have unlimited time, I'll discover which safety features were dismantled or adjusted in order to give you these parts, and in fact which parts you stole."

Michelle kept her facial expression neutral. Of course she was bound to have made mistakes, miscalculations, and of course bureaucrats were relentless in their sacred mission of enforcing any and all regulations and controlling every aspect of human behavior. Fortunately her schedule was such that she only needed to consider temporary damage control.

"Now why would I waste my time with that?" she asked reasonably. "I have too much to do as it is, keeping this settlement and its habitats functional. What would I do with equipment I stole? Sell it? No one is interested in money here."

"That's the only thing I don't know yet," Himmelsbeck admitted. "And you'll definitely keep me from finding out exactly what you're doing, at least as long as you are here. So the obvious solution is to send you back to Earth on the next transport spaceship. Law enforcement there can decide what to do with you, and I can tear apart your living and working quarters, piece by piece, until I find the answers."

"The obvious solution," he repeated, tapping his fingers on her monitor table.

Maybe Himmelsbeck had no idea of her motives, but his became immediately clear to her. The slimy little functionary wanted in on the action; he wanted a cut. This would make things considerably easier.

"And the not so obvious solution," she asked.

"You don't have any plan," he said. "You've been pilfering odds and ends of stuff with no plan for further distribution. Maybe you're a kleptomaniac or maybe you just get your jollies sabotaging sensible safety regulations. Either way, sooner or later you will need help in moving your loot."

"Hmm," Michelle said noncommittally.

"And things are changing," Himmelsbeck looked directly into her eyes. "It's no longer about pure survival here on Mars. People have developed, to varying degrees, a taste for luxury. They are willing to transfer assets on Earth to acquire non-regulation items here on Mars."

"And you have the contacts to make this possible?" Michelle asked.

Himmelsbeck stretched out in her chair. "Right now I picture a one-person-operation, and I'll keep it that way for a long time. However, I see possibilities of taking you on as an employee to our mutual benefit."

"Right," Michelle thought. "I steal for you, and you can always threaten to reveal my actions. At least I've managed to look stupid enough for you to fool even though I obviously made mistakes." Sigh. She hadn't had enough respect for Murphy's Law.

She smiled, hoping that her face had the required helpless, little girl look on it. "Well, Mr. Himmelsbeck, you have definitely given me a lot to think about. I know when I'm outclassed, so of course I'm willing to enter a new working relationship. But it's a professional obsession with us engineers; I need to consider details. Why don't you come around tomorrow, I'll show you what I've acquired, and we'll pound out an agreement. Can I rely on your discretion in the meantime?"

Mr. Himmelsbeck stood up and smiled unpleasantly as he left. "My thoughts precisely. May I say that it is a pleasure to deal with such a pragmatic individual."

Michelle returned to her undocumented storeroom and activated the team of rocket robots. Her schedule was being rushed by a few sols, but this was manageable. The robots had the compartments of her one-person rocket assembled and stocked within a few hours. She had indeed managed to steal everything she needed to make and supply her own rocket so she could explore the universe beyond this puny star system while everyone else spent the rest of their lives obeying regulations on Mars.

She was especially proud of her AI equipment, things she had designed and tested for months. She would be able to control communications systems on Mars and Earth until she was far into the Oort Cloud. Her nimble little spaceship would allow her to land on small astronomical bodies to replenish any materials the nanobots would need to keep her alive and speeding.

She accompanied the robots to the rocket station where they snapped all the pieces together and she had a functional rocket ready to go. She and the robots ran several system analysis inspections, relying however on double redundancy. The rocket now had everything she would need for her journey. She wiped the robots' memories and led them back to her workshop.

There she made the necessary adjustments to her secret storeroom. It now contained supplies and life support systems for at least one Martian year and was fairly undetectable, i.e. electromagnetic waves couldn't penetrate the walls from any direction. Once the fake wall slid over the entrance, no one could suspect that this room existed.

This was satisfactory. She was a thief, not a murderer.

Mr. Himmelsbeck showed up smirking an hour later.

"Let me show you my stash, and you tell me what kind of profit you can organize for us," Michelle said as she led him to the secret storeroom.

"Wow," he said as he entered the room. "I never thought you had so much, and I had no idea this place existed. You've got a whole warehouse in here."

He seemed occupied, so Michelle said softly, "Look around. I think I'll go change into something more comfortable."

"What," Himmelsbeck said, raising a gray eyebrow. "You are full of surprises." But then he headed to the back of the warehouse, running his greedy fingers along the shelves.

Michelle indeed changed into something more comfortable for her trip, a fully functional spacesuit. She returned to the storeroom, sealed the door, and tapped on the monitor on the wall. The room filled with the gas she calculated would render Mr. Himmelsbeck unconscious for a few hours. Once he was lying on the floor, she went in and placed a book of instructions and recommendations on his chest. With a little hard work and creative thought he should be able to escape after a few Martian months. Then, of course, he would be free to make whatever profit he could from the things she left behind.

Michelle, however, had to take advantage of this window of opportunity and leave the planet. Finally, after so many years of learning and serving, she was on her way to escape the limitations of the star system she happened to be born in. Humans were meant to leave their safe homes and explore the unknown, and she had created this chance for herself.

Technically she didn't even feel like a thief, just an efficient engineer. Other humans on Earth and Mars would certainly benefit from the data she gathered on her way to Proxima Centauri. She hoped they would follow her lead.

ABOUT THE AUTHOR

Mary Jo Rabe grew up on a farm in eastern Iowa, got degrees from Michigan State University (German and math) and University of Wisconsin-Milwaukee (library science) where she became a late-blooming science fiction reader and writer. She worked in the library of the chancery office of the Archdiocese of Freiburg, Germany for 41 years, and lives with her husband in Titisee-Neustadt, Germany.

She has had stories accepted for Fiction River and Pulphouse. She has published "Blue Sunset", inspired by Spoon River Anthology and The Martian Chronicles, electronically and has had poems and stories published in Space Opera Mashup (Curated Anthologies), Alternate Hilarities, Pandora, Stygian Articles, The Martian Wave, Astropoetica, The Sword Review, Raven Electrick, Mindflights, and Space and Time.

Personal blog: https://maryjorabe.wordpress.com/ Publishing blog: https://teedsgalaxypress.wordpress.com Website: http://www.-teedsgalaxypress.com

She indulges in sporadic activity on Facebook and Twitter

THE RAKENTENRUCKSACK SABOTAGE

DeAnna Knippling

Johann Sauer came to the United States in 1947 via Operation Paperclip after World War II. Over sixteen hundred scientists and engineers were recruited, including Werner von Braun and his V-2 rocket team. Many of these men were former members, if not leaders, of the Nazi party. These scientists were also instrumental in developing the rockets used in space programs. It was one of those things that if we hadn't taken up those men, the Russians would have—and in fact tried to do so. The race for space started during the cleanup of World War II.

Herr Sauer was the kind of beautiful, charming blond man of early-middle years that one likes to see along the street. He was always well-dressed in his tailored suits and had frequented the intellectual clubs and cabarets of cosmopolitan Berlin in the 1920s and 1930s, discussing philosophy and technology over coffees, listening to jazz (he was of course present during the visit of Josephine Baker in 1925, who called the city "jewel-like"), dancing with the girls in their beaded dresses, and making his name in the science of rocketry.

While von Braun and his team worked on the V-2 rockets at Peenemünde, Sauer and his team worked on another program: the personal rocket propulsion unit, or der Raketenrucksack.

Two models were to be developed. The first would be simply a sort of heavy brace or belt containing minimal fuel, which would be used by paratroopers—die Fallschirmjäger—to control their descent.

The second model, which resembled a heavy backpack with braces for the feet and armatures for the arms and wrists, would be used to maneuver from a ground-based position on the battlefield. The soldier would be able to leap over the existing lines and do damage from behind. Then he would abandon the rocketpack, which would consume its remaining fuel in a triggered, timed explosion.

Neither version had been put into use before the end of the war.

The reason for this was that, inevitably, illogically, no matter what was done to prevent it, the models would explode during testing. The paratroopers testing the smaller, simpler unit would successfully maneuver their drops onto the most precise targets—then find that their rocketpacks would explode upon impact. Even the gentlest of landings proved to be too severe.

It was thought for a time that the paratroopers, who were prisoners of war promised freedom upon successfully testing the equipment, were sabotaging the tests. But after several volunteers from the Luftwaffe gave their lives in disproving this theory, plans were put on hold.

Of what happened to the men testing the second, more sophisticated, model, it is not necessary to speak. Again, Sauer used prisoners of war to perform his testing. As far as he was concerned, it was as expedient as using animals for the testing of women's cosmetics.

Unfortunate, but well-intentioned.

Sauer's lack of success did not weigh upon him greatly: he had survived the war without injury to himself. He was that kind of man. However, before the end, the SS had raided his department and found two scientists of hidden Jewish ancestry, a situation that the officers did not hesitate to ameliorate in the most expedient manner possible. The scientists were blamed for the failures, and Sauer reprimanded for not performing a more diligent search into the men's backgrounds. But by then, it was too late: die Raketen-rucksäcke could not be produced en masse for the war effort, even if they had been successfully tested. The necessary resources had already been spent.

Later, it was said that Sauer had known of the men's ancestry and had looked aside both from their presence and from their mysteriously effective sabotage. This rumor stood him in good stead in America, especially after he was brought in 1951 to Huntsville, Alabama, to work his magic upon the rocketry program there.

His magic was just as ineffective in Huntsville as it was in Peenemünde.

I was called in from Hampton, Virginia, to determine what the problem was. The blueprints had already been reviewed, the figures had already been checked.

I had little hope of being able to turn either of the Raketenruck-sack models into something useful. In my opinion, it was damned foolishness to ask a man to leap behind enemy lines and expect him to essentially perform the function of human bomb. It would be better to focus the efforts of the scientists toward developing peace-time technologies, in my opinion. If the more modest Raketenruck-sack models could be developed to be used in space to help maneuver without use of gravity, that would be the better invest-ment—in my opinion.

Johann Sauer knew my opinions on the matter. We were at odds with each other before I even arrived.

But he dutifully escorted me through the project. I saw where the materials were being developed and tested. I saw the computers calculating the data on how far the Raketenrucksack would carry an operator of such-and-such a weight. I saw the stored prototypes, of which there were several. I saw the testing area, where men were strapped into lighter or heavier frameworks and made to try to walk about, or bend over, or lift and aim a rifle with the armatures fastened about their forearms.

I did not see any direct testing of the Raketenrucksack's rockets.

"Who are the men doing the testing for you?" I asked. They were all men of color, and I already knew—and Sauer knew that I knew—the answer.

"They come from a nearby prison," he admitted. "The security concerns of dealing with such men have been thoroughly dealt with. There should be no fear of them escaping, or of harming anyone."

"There is always some chance of them sabotaging the equipment," I said. "That is the problem. In Germany, you would use prisoners of war, men who would rather die than see your program succeed, no?"

Sauer smiled at me, the charming grin of a man who is fantasizing murder. "That is so. But the men were closely supervised then, as they are now. And, of course, in Germany we tested the equipment with men whose loyalty was never questioned. It was a great tragedy."

"I have reviewed your entire design, manufacturing, and testing process, except for that final step," said I. "I maintain that the design itself is flawless—"

Sauer thanked me for that.

"—and that the manufacture is within all possible tolerances. As the great detective once said, 'When you have eliminated the impossible, whatever remains, however improbable, must be the truth.' It is the testing process itself that is flawed."

"It is closely monitored, I tell you."

"Are you saying that the Raketenrucksacks are ready? That their testing has been an unmitigated success? Because that is what you seem to be saying. There are no issues with the units, and they should be employed immediately."

Still smiling, Sauer replied that that was not his meaning. I asked him what he meant, then, by saying that it was impossible that the error could be in the process that he so completely controlled.

He said, "Are you saying that it is I who is at fault?"

"I am saying that it is my duty to investigate every aspect of the production of these machines, and that you seem to be preventing me from fulfilling this duty, which I have duly reported."

Here Sauer's smiled faltered.

"I have already sent an initial report to my superiors," I clarified. It does not do well to trust former Nazis not to solve a situation such as I presented in the most convenient way. I had no intention of disappearing into one of the swamps outside Huntsville, burn marks at the back of my shattered skull.

Visibly shuddering with frustration, Sauer said, "I do not wish to say that. I only wish to say that I cannot conceive of what the problem might be."

"Then we shall review the testing process."

"I had wished to spare you of it."

"It is not my duty to be spared of anything."

With that, we proceeded to a second testing area, completely separated from the first. We had to take a car to the second facility, a large corrugated steel shed that seemed to have been made of patchwork shades of olive and tan. The smell made me recollect several unpleasant incidents from the war. As for myself, I had served different masters than Herr Sauer.

Inside the shed I could clearly identify the aroma of the slaughterhouse. The stains on the steel walls and damaged cement floor had been sprayed down with water, but not scrubbed. It was driven home to me once again that the testing of the Raketenrucksacks in the United States had not been a success.

After a careful search of the facilities, I asked, "When are the units brought here for testing? They do not appear to be stored here."

"Are we in agreement that any sabotage could not have occurred here?" Sauer demanded with an arrogant sweep of his arm.

"We are in agreement about nothing, until I write my final report," I answered. "Please answer the question."

"The units are brought here only at the last moment."

"Are they ever left unsupervised?"

"The testers are not left unsupervised.

"That was not the question I asked."

Sauer called the driver over to us. "Explain to Mr. Morgenthau how die Raketenrucksäcke are handled, when they are brought here for testing."

The driver said, "We watch the prisoners very closely, Herr Morgenthau."

"I wish to know about the units, not the men," I said.

"All our men are trustworthy," Sauer said. "Their loyalty is unquestionable."

"Yet I would like to see how the handling of the machines is done," I said.

Laboriously and thoroughly, the driver walked me through the process, first showing me how the men were handled and secured. It was as Sauer had stated: the handling was very secure, with two men keeping their eyes on the prisoner at all times.

The unit was left in the rear of a specially-fitted truck, in which it was secured and cushioned from damage. It was not until after the prisoner had been brought into the shed and secured with a chain and manacle to the wall that the unit was removed from the truck and brought inside, where it was then filled with the current fuel mixture, which was brought in a separate, pressurized container within the truck.

"Who guards the unit and the container while the prisoner is being moved?" I asked.

"Who guards it? The driver of the truck does," our driver said. "Whoever is assigned that day. It varies."

"Have you ever driven the truck?"

"I have," he said.

"Show me how the guarding is supposed to be done," I ordered.

We play-acted the routine. The driver was to exit the cab of the truck and stand next to the rear end of the truck—we marked the outline of where the truck would park in the gravel before the shed—until called for. I told the driver to stand near the rear of the truck, then began my search.

I did not find what I was looking for within easy distance of the driver, and widened my circle.

But it was not until I circled the corner of the shed that I discovered what I was looking for: cigarette butts.

The drivers, of course, did not wish to stand next to such dangerous fuel when they smoked, and had walked around the corner to do it.

"You smoke?" I asked the driver softly.

His face had gone pale and erupted in beads of sweat. He nodded. I did not call attention to this. Sauer, on the other hand, in observing my search, had turned a frightful shade of scarlet, and was clearly restraining himself from screaming at the driver.

I took Sauer aside and said, "You must maintain all appearance of calm. We may be watched, even now, by the saboteur or saboteurs."

This caused the boiling rage to subside, at least somewhat.

"Who did you think is doing it?" he asked. "It is almost as though they followed me from Germany."

I agreed with him, but said that it would be unlikely. "Who, besides the other scientists who accompanied you, would have done so?"

He shook his head. His failure of imagination was, at least, consistent. "I cannot imagine that my colleagues would do such a thing."

"Are there any other members of your old team in Peenemünde who are here in Huntsville? Any at all?"

He named several men, who had been removed to other departments.

"We will begin our search there," I said, ignoring his denials that his colleagues could possibly have done such a thing. "But first..."

❀

I sat in the back of the Jeep, my hands handcuffed. A guard sat on either side of me with a loaded weapon. I was saying a prayer under my breath. This, too, was a kind of test. Of my own nerve, if nothing else.

A second vehicle drove behind us, the truck containing the fuel and the machine. Nothing about the machine, truck, or fuel had been changed. A second guard had accompanied the driver. If one or the other of them were prompted to smoke while the guards in the first car dealt with me, then they could go around the corner—but only one at a time.

I was escorted inside the shed and manacled to the wall. I wore only what the prisoners wore, a simple brown uniform. Not even my own shoes were allowed to me. I was indeed heavily guarded.

The Raketenrucksack was brought in by the driver, who carried it on his back. It was the second model, the heavier, more dangerous type.

I was strapped into it. It was a curious feeling. I did not feel the weight of it so much as the loss of balance, for the fuel tank that had been built into the back was supported by the struts attached to my legs, a clever mechanism that allowed me to bend my knees enough to walk, but that supported the weight of the heavy tank. But that weight still pulled me backward, and I necessarily had to lean forward in order to keep from toppling over. I said as much to Sauer, who smiled charmingly and assured me that they were working on it.

I said, "I do not wish to fly up into the air and crash into the roof of the shed, but only see that the machine does not explode when it is activated."

"Are you sure you wish to do this?" Sauer asked.

"If I am killed, it will disprove my theory—and no blame will attach to you," I said. "Unless, of course, you are the one who is sabotaging the machinery." I had cleverly substituted two men of my personal acquaintance for the driver and guard of the truck, who had assured me by signs that no one had tampered with the machinery once they begun to watch it.

"What we normally do is attach a piece of twine to this switch in the back of the unit," Sauer said. "Then we remove ourselves from the shed and pull it. If all goes well, then you will rise about a foot, then fall again. In case you are not instantly killed, you must be careful not to lose your balance, and to keep your knees bent as you land."

"Then that it how I wish to do it," I said.

Once again, he asked me if I was certain of my intentions. He had never yet seen a successful testing of the machine. His words were such that, if I went only by them, I should have thought him the most concerned and solicitous of men. His tone, however, belied his state of mind. He was very nearly suppressing a sense of glee at my impending death.

"This is how I wish it to be done," I said.

The men retreated from the shed, trailing a length of twine.

I, being a free man rather than a prisoner, was instructed to give them a count of three, and tell them when to pull the piece of twine.

"One...two...three...now!"

I felt a jerk at my back, and then I was flying. I rose into the air, clutching the grips of the armatures, which had been welded in place on the prototype so that the operator could not make any adjustments to the angles of the fuel jets. I laughed aloud with joy.

Then, almost as soon as it had begun, I began to sink. I feared to move, lest the rockets tilt and cause me to smash headfirst into the corrugated steel before me.

I bent my knees as I landed, and came to a rest making hysterical whoops of laughter. I had lived.

The men released me from the straps. I said, "That was the most incredible experience I have ever had. If there is any more fuel, Sauer, you simply must try it for yourself. It is a miracle."

The two men who had come with me appeared shaken. "Boss, if it's all right with you, we're going to go have that smoke now." They had both stayed on guard the entire time.

"If you don't mind, I'll come with you," I said. My legs were shaking. I said, "I would say that my theory has been confirmed, wouldn't you, Herr Sauer?"

He made no answer. They were already strapping him into the machine.

I gave him a cheerful wave. The three of us walked away from the shed, saying nothing but giving each other looks. Suddenly, we all heard, but muted by the distance, the sound of iron banging off of cement, then a few curses in German.

They are very fast, you know. We had seen them as gray streaks during the fighting, working against first one side, then the other. They were legendary.

And, apparently, they found die Raketenrucksäcke so offensive that they could not allow them ever to be used. I cannot say that I ever discovered the logic of the situation—to allow the giant rockets to be built during the V-2 program in Germany, but not die Raketenrucksäcke? But they used to attack our planes as often as they did the Germans'. Clearly, we men understood little of them. Their logic was their own.

I suspected—prayed—that it was Herr Sauer himself with whom they had taken offense. Perhaps he had stolen something from them, or killed someone of whom they were fond. I did not know.

As for myself, it was his smile that offended me. That such a man should be able to smile so gaily after what he had done. That he should be allowed to continue to do it.

And so, I took a risk, all of it balanced on the most delicate supposition.

Faintly, we heard him call, "One...two...three...now!"

Then the explosion. We returned to the shed, at speed.

One wall had been cast away from the building's frame. The two guards lived, but not the driver, who had been impaled by a fragment of steel from the machine, through the heart.

Of what happened to Herr Sauer, it is not necessary to speak.

We returned to the truck to radio for help. From the radio dial hung a ring which proved to be Sauer's wedding band. Had he been wearing it earlier? I could not be certain, although I was later assured that he never removed it.

As I said, they are fast, those gremlins.

I returned to Virginia to face an inquiry on the matter, and said nothing of my suspicions. The program was closed soon after the end of the inquiry, and never reopened.

In return, I found that my vehicles were always in good order. The only time I ever had any car trouble was once on a dark night, when I saw something gray streak across the road, and swerved to miss it.

ABOUT THE AUTHOR

DeAnna Knippling loves all things Gothic and pulp. You can find her writing all kinds of science fiction, fantasy, horror, and crime fiction at www.WonderlandPress.com

THE LEVITATION ENGINES

The frosted glass doors of the elevator slid open onto the wide dock that jutted out in the sky several stories above ground level. Astrid flinched as Dagmar, her six-year-old niece, squealed at the sight of the elliptical shapes of the airships hovering high above them. Boat-like wooden crafts, each with a varying number of metal propellers along the sides, hung suspended from each of the dirigibles by ropes and cables. They floated in the open air just off the dock, moored by thick ropes that ran from each craft and attached to large, iron rings. Sections of sturdy railings lined the edge of the dock in between each of the spots where a ship was tied up.

Astrid rubbed her ears, took a deep breath of the familiar scents of metal, hemp, and sun-warmed pine, and adjusted the straps of the pack slung over her left shoulder. She had the day off from the family business, where she designed clockwork creatures—birds, butterflies, bees, and the like—for rich people to purchase and play with. She'd planned on spending her day testing the levitation engines she'd been working on in secret, not minding a small child. But her older sister hadn't expected to go into labor for a few more weeks, and Erika's carefully thought-out plans for child care had all been predicated on the baby arriving after the Midsummer Festival, not before.

She'd braided her long hair and put on a short-sleeved blouse and a pair of trousers that morning, thinking she'd be spending her day cleaning and oiling metal, cutting gears and sprockets, and adjusting timing devices instead of entertaining her niece. At least no one here at the dock would turn up their nose at her attire, like people would in most other parts of the city. There were plenty of female airship captains and crewmembers, and even the most judgmental people realized that it didn't make any sense to wear a skirt while working on a ship where you might need to rope up and climb overboard to adjust a propeller or something.

Her niece, who had kept up a stream of high-pitched chatter since Astrid picked her up that morning, had—thankfully—become uncharacteristically quiet. The child slipped a tiny, somewhat sticky hand into her aunt's palm as they stepped out of the elevator and began to walk down the long, wide, rectangular dock. Astrid's thick boots made soft clomping sounds on the thick, wooden boards; Dagmar padded alongside in her sandals, the light summer breeze ruffling the lace trim on her blue-and-white cotton frock. Her dark brown curls bounced on her shoulders as she turned from side to side to look at the ships as they walked past, and her hazel eyes were as wide as saucers. She was awfully cute, but taking care of a child was a surprising amount of work. Astrid hadn't realized just how much work until today, and she'd only been watching Dagmar for a few hours.

Why anyone thought having children was a good idea at all, much less having five of them, was beyond her. She'd much rather spend her time designing clockwork machinery. And now, thanks to Erika and baby number six—or at least it was hopefully only one baby this time, since the last two had turned out to be sets of twins —she was going to have to wait another week to get back to her experiment.

Astrid had designed a pair of mechanical fans that, if attached to another object, would—or at least should—propel it into the air. The initial test hadn't gone very well. She'd attached the engines to a heavy wooden chair, one on each side. They'd lifted the chair ten or so feet off the ground, but then one engine failed, and everything plummeted to the ground. At least the chair hadn't been badly damaged, but she'd learned her lesson, and had been thinking through reasonably plausible stories just in case something went wrong in her next experiment.

Astrid didn't think anything would go wrong. She'd cleaned and oiled the gears until the silver gleamed and the copper shone like burnished sunshine. She might, of course, run out of fuel, but that was an entirely different problem. She'd snuck tiny bits of the fuel used to power the automatons two of her uncles worked on, until she'd siphoned enough for a few tests. The levitation engines didn't need much fuel once they got started, but she hadn't yet figured out how to keep the gears turning indefinitely, so the current design required more than she'd like. But she'd work on that issue once she'd verified the engines truly worked.

They paused for a few moments to look at a gondola that had a large metal rudder jutting out of its stern, and then continued on. It was the middle of the afternoon, and the airship dock was relatively quiet. The cargo ships generally arrived before noon, and it looked like they'd already all been unloaded, based on the number of crates and barrels that stood in the middle of the dock.

Things would pick up again in a few hours when the wealthy returned from day trips to the shore and headed home to wash off the scents of sand and salt and sunshine. Later in the evening they'd board ships to ferry them across town for an evening of dancing and dining at the palace, or simply float high above the city. They'd sip sparkling wine while gazing down at the twinkling lights of the wrought iron gas lamps that lined the cobblestoned streets, oblivious to—or unconcerned about—the fact that the less well-off were walking along those very streets as they made their ways home from the factory district.

Astrid's family wasn't poor, but they weren't rich, either. Her parents and aunt and uncles had teamed up to form the clockwork business before she was born. While it was a successful enterprise, the revenue was not only shared among the entire family, but they also donated a good percentage to help people in need.

She'd learned to steer clear of their customers, most of whom were not anywhere close to being in need, whenever possible. She occasionally had to meet with a well-to-do woman who wanted Astrid to design a mechanical beetle for her cat to chase, or a man who'd decided he wanted to keep a flock of tiny clockwork birds in his top hat to surprise people at parties. Occasionally she'd find herself working on a project commissioned by one of the city's wizards, who apparently enjoyed the novelty of having a plaything powered by mechanics instead of magic.

The technical challenges of these projects were fun and interesting, but she often had to bite her lip to keep from scolding these people about using their money for such trivial things, when so many others struggled to put food on the table.

Unlike the beautiful toys she designed for the wealthy, the levitation engines were designed to help others. She'd seen people who worked at the city factories moving goods and equipment end up with back problems so bad they eventually became unable to work at all. Her goal was to create a mechanical contraption that could be used to move heavy things from place to place. Whether the levitation engines would work for that purpose, she didn't yet know. But she did know that they weren't commissioned by someone for a frivolous reason. She'd just have to wait another week or so for the opportunity to try them out again.

She wrinkled her nose and strode across the wide, wooden planks of the airship dock, pulling her awestruck niece along behind her.

"How do they stay in the air?" Dagmar asked in her tinny, high-pitched voice.

"Mathematics," Astrid said, wending her way through the barrels and boxes that were piled in the middle of this section of the dock. She started as something small, sparkly, and bright green flew by, zooming past mere inches from her left shoulder. It darted behind a stack of wooden whiskey barrels.

"What was that?" Dagmar asked.

"Just some kind of bird," Astrid said, although she wasn't sure it had been at all. What kind of bird was that brilliant shade of green, and had a long, thin tail? It had looked for all the world like a miniature dragon. Not that she'd ever seen one in person, of course, and she wanted to keep it that way. Prickles ran down the back of her neck. "We've looked at the ships for long enough. Let's head over to the park."

"I think it was a dragon," Dagmar said. She slipped her hand out of Astrid's and trotted over to the whiskey barrels.

Astrid clenched her jaw and started after her niece.

"Let's go, Dagmar," she said, her voice taut. She reached out to grab her niece's shoulder and then jumped back as a brilliant white bolt of light zapped one of the barrels next to her, knocking it to the ground. Whiskey began to gurgle out of the hole that had been burned in the side of container. Dagmar shrieked and ducked behind a crate.

Astrid threw a glance over her shoulder and froze as she saw a man and a woman dressed in crimson and gold ran toward her, each waving a wand. The man pointed his wand at something behind Astrid; another bolt of light shot from it, narrowly missing her left arm.

"It's mine!" someone cried from behind her.

She whipped around to see a scowling man dressed in red running toward them from the opposite direction. Blue light shot from his wand and hit the floor of the dock near her, sparks flying as the energy seared a hole through the thick wooden boards.

Whatever the small, green creature had been, it appeared it was being chased by a bunch of battling wizards.

Astrid dashed over to the crate Dagmar had scurried behind,

and flung herself around the corner just as a bolt of energy hit the side of the crate. She held her pack up to shield her face as splinters of pine flew into the air, and then lowered it and opened her eyes as the pieces of wood settled.

She stood in a space maybe an arm's width wide in between two rows of wooden crates that had been stacked several times her height. Straight in front of her she could see the dark brown shape of a gondola behind the thick railing on the eastern edge of the dock. The boat swayed slightly as the wind tugged at the airship that floated in the sky above it.

Dagmar was nowhere to be seen.

Astrid ran down the narrow aisle between the stacks of crates and out into the bright sunshine. There weren't any crates or boxes or anything nearby for Dagmar to have hidden behind. Would she have gone to the other side of the dock? That would have meant heading toward the fighting wizards, and even a six-year-old would realize that was a bad idea. One of the wizards must have shot a bolt of electricity this way and severed three of the four ropes that moored the nearest boat to the dock. The wind had picked up, and the airship was tugging the polished wooden gondola, bumping it gently into the railing.

She bit her lip, adjusted the strap of her pack, and walked down the dock, but she didn't see any place where a small child could hide. She threw a glance over her shoulder. The occasional shout or bolt of energy showed that the wizards' fight continued, but it appeared to be localized to the western side of the dock. For now, at least. She'd never seen wizards behave like that before, and wasn't sure if the dockmaster or a constable would even be able to break up the strange, magical fight.

"Aunt Astrid?"

She spun around to see Dagmar's little face peeking over the edge of the gondola attached to the severed ropes just as the last rope gave way. The boat began to rise up from the dock, carried by the airship that floated above it.

"No!" Astrid sprinted toward the boat, but the wind had picked up, and the craft had moved too far away from the dock for her to reach it. She stared at it for a moment, her heart racing, and then ran to the next boat and tugged at one of the knots that tied it to the mooring ring. Out of the corner of her eye she could see Dagmar's airship drifting far away, moving quickly thanks to the afternoon breeze.

After a few minutes she managed to start to loosen the first knot—but there were three more after this one. At the speed Dagmar's airship was going, it would be gone from sight by the time she got the next ship in the air. The winds were blowing her niece out to sea. She'd have to find someone to help. Maybe if the dockmaster sent all the airships after Dagmar they could catch her. But they'd have to do so soon, or she'd be so far from land that it would be impossible to tell which direction her airship had gone.

Astrid rose to her feet, wincing as the metal of the levitation engines in her pack bumped against her side, and then she gasped as she realized there was one thing that might help her get to Dagmar in time.

She knelt down and pulled the engines out of her pack. The bright copper of the casing flashed in the sunshine. Hooks on the sides of each engine were attached to lengths of rope that she'd tied to the rails of the chair when she'd done her single experiment. The pieces of rope were short, but they were long enough to wrap around her body. She positioned the engines so they sat just below her shoulder blades, and tied the rope in knots as tightly as she could. She took a deep breath, tucked the bag that had held the engines into the waistband of her trousers, and then switched the engines on.

She shot up into the sky so fast her stomach felt as though it had been turned upside-down. The engines hummed softly as their gears spun. She reached behind her back with both hands and turned the dials down on both engines. That slowed her momentum until she stopped moving up, and instead hovered so high above the dock she must look like a bird if anyone glanced up.

Off in the distance she could see Dagmar's airship, a tiny shape on the horizon to the east. She needed to move horizontally, not vertically! She'd designed the levitation engines to lift things up and down, not sideways. She'd planned on putting together more controls once she'd refined the basics, but the project was so new that she hadn't done more than think about how she might enhance the system if it turned out to actually work.

She gritted her teeth and bent forward at an angle that caused the engines to turn so they'd point toward the east and, hopefully, propel her in that direction instead of straight up. This worked, but she found herself moving both laterally and downward, because the engines no longer provided sufficient lift. She turned the dials up higher, but discovered if she turned them up too far she'd start rising up in the air again, and would lose the horizontal movement. She fiddled with the dials, and kept twisting and turning, until she found a setting that allowed her to stretch her body out as if she were swimming through the air and propelled her forward. As long as she stayed in this position, she moved reasonably fast in a horizontal direction without changing her altitude.

The gears in the engine made a soft whirring as they turned, almost like the sound of a bunch of bees buzzing around. The afternoon sun felt warm and soothing on her shoulders, and the breeze ruffled the tiny bits of hair that had escaped from her long braids. She was still far away from Dagmar's airship, which the wind had carried past the shore and out above the ocean, but she was closing in on it. She'd gained so much altitude that she was much higher in the air than the airship, but at her current rate of speed it looked like she'd reach it in another fifteen minutes or so, and now that she'd figured out how to adjust the gears she knew she'd just have to change her position and lower the setting to drop down when she reached the boat. She took a deep breath, relaxing for the first time since they'd encountered the strange, green creature and the wizards who were chasing it. She was going to reach the airship and save her niece.

And...the levitation engines worked!

She'd designed them with the intent of providing an automated way to move heavy objects about, so that people who worked at the city factories didn't have to strain their backs moving boxes and crates and things. Now it was clear they'd work for that purpose— with a little more testing and customization, of course. But it was also clear that they could be used for something she'd never even thought of in her wildest dreams.

Flying.

Astrid had flow in airships before, but that experience was nothing compared to gliding through the air like this. Other than the soft hum of the gears turning, the sky was quiet. She gazed down at the green, rolling hills that lay far below her. Houses and barns were scattered here and there, linked by the thin, curving ribbon of paved stones that made up the road that ran from the city to the seaside. Groves of trees covered the low hills and clustered along the banks of a small river. The tiny brown and white shapes of horses dotted stretches of green grass.

Dark chunks of rock lined the edge of the beach, forming low cliffs that dropped on to the white, gleaming expanse of sand. And then she was over the water. She breathed in the salty tang of the ocean, and watched as the ocean grew darker and deeper the further out she flew from shore. This must be what birds felt like, soaring high above the earth and the waves. It was calm. Beautiful. Peaceful.

The left levitation engine gave a loud clang and shuddered to a stop as its gears seized up. Astrid gasped as she began to lose altitude. She reached behind to turn the dial on the right engine as far up as it would go, and breathed a sigh as she stopped dropping and leveled out. She was maybe fifty feet above the airship, and a hundred feet away. Ninety. Eighty. She was going to make it!

The right engine sputtered and its gears began to slow.

It had run out of fuel.

Astrid's heart thumped. She spread her arms wide, as if they were wings, and angled toward the ship. If she was lucky, she could use her height and momentum to reach the ship. Maybe. She held her breath and focused on the shapes of the airship and its gondola as she fell forward through the air, plummeting toward the ship—or, if things went wrong, toward the ocean—faster than she ever would have thought possible.

She reached her arms as she approached the ship, and managed to wrap her right arm around one of the ropes that connected the airship to the gondola. She pulled her arm tight, holding the rope in the crook of her elbow. She grabbed the rope with her left hand and slid down it to the ship, trying to ignore the pain as thick rope dug into her bare skin. She reached the railing and clung to the rope for a moment before falling to the wooden deck. She lay there for a moment, her eyes closed, and her breaths coming in great gasps. She'd made it!

After her breath slowed, she opened her eyes to see Dagmar's tiny face looking down at her.

"Aunt Astrid, I didn't know you could fly," Dagmar said.

"Neither did I," Astrid said, her voice cracking. She pushed herself up on one elbow, and then froze. Next to her niece stood a small, green, miniature dragon, its golden eyes the color of the sun.

Astrid swallowed. She'd never seen one before, but this creature was unmistakably a dragon. Were dragons good? Bad? She wasn't sure.

She stood up and untied the ropes strapping the levitation engines to her back, wincing as she bumped the area of skin the rope had rubbed raw. She pulled her pack out of her waistband and slid the engines inside.

"Harald can fly too," Dagmar said. "He's sorry we got caught up with those wizards that were chasing him. But he's glad, too, because otherwise he and I wouldn't have met, and now we're best friends."

"Okay," Astrid said. She was at a loss for how to respond. She set the pack on the deck of the ship and eyed the little dragon.

"He can talk, but no one else can hear him," Dagmar said. "Just me. He says to tell you he's pleased to meet you. And thank you for coming to save me, because he doesn't know how to fly an airship, and he's too little to carry me."

"Nice to, um, meet you, Harald," Astrid said.

Harald bowed his head, as if he understood her. His scales sparkled in the late afternoon sunlight.

Was he actually speaking to Dagmar? What would being a dragon's friend have to do with being able to hear it speak?

Astrid blinked as she realized the implications of what her niece had just said.

"Dagmar, did Harald use the word familiar?"

Dagmar nodded. "That's what I said. He's my familiar. My best friend."

The wizards chasing Harald had been trying to catch him because they each wanted the dragon to be their familiar. And now Harald was Dagmar's familiar.

Normal people didn't have familiars.

But wizards did.

This was probably not what Erika had had in mind when she'd asked Astrid to watch Dagmar for a few days.

Astrid took a deep breath. Having a wizard in the family was going to be interesting. Were there schools for wizard children? Or did they need private tutors? She was glad she'd be able to hand Dagmar—and Harald—back to Erika soon.

Although perhaps Erika could use the help. And maybe Dagmar could as well.

"I'd better turn us around," she said. She walked over to the control panel and turned the wheel. The airship began to make a slow, wide curve back toward the city. Whoever owned the ship probably thought it was lost forever and would be happy to get it back. The rogue wizards should be dealt with by now, and even if they were upset about Harald, there was nothing they could do about him now. Wizards and familiars bonded for life.

She glanced at her niece. Dagmar and Harald had curled up together in a corner of the deck, and it looked like Dagmar was having trouble keeping her eyes open. The little dragon rested his chin on the little girl's shoulder. His bright green wings were furled.

Wings...

Of course—the next phase of her project would be to build herself wings! That way if both levitation engines failed she'd be able to glide down to earth. Dragon wings would be a good example to use as a model, as they didn't have feathers like birds did.

She had no doubt now that that the engines would be able to levitate heavy objects and help the workers in the city's factories. She'd just need to experiment with the motors to get them to support enough weight, and would have to work out a much better control mechanism.

But there was no reason she couldn't also work on a design for a personal levitation system as well. In addition to wings as a backup system, goggles would be helpful if you were flying into the sun. And a harness would be much more reliable—not to mention comfortable—than using rope to tie engines to your back.

Astrid grinned. She had a lot of experimenting—and a lot of flying—to do.

ABOUT THE AUTHOR

Jamie focuses on getting into the minds and hearts of her characters, whether she's writing about a saloon girl in the Old West, a man who discovers the barista he's in love with is a naiad, or a ghost who haunts the house she was killed in—even though that house no longer exists.

Jamie lives in Colorado and spends her free time in a futile quest to wear out her two border collies, since she hasn't given in and gotten them their own herd of sheep. Yet.

COLLISION NUMBER ONE

Kelly Cairo

"When am I going under?" Captain Madeline Kaze asked. Her words slurred a little bit, and her voice sounded strangely scratchy.

In fact, everything seemed a bit off. A moment ago, the ship's lab was a busy place – engineers passing portable leak detectors over every inch of the freeze booths, doctors taking last minute readings and blood samples from the crew before they went under, and technicians administering final doses of "cryo-goo" – and now it was nearly silent. Just the hum of the air filters.

All the booths were sealed, looking like row after row of shiny silver missiles but for the rectangular peep-holes at eye level. The lab was dim, except for the area around Kaze's booth. The main bank of control panels blinked amber and green messages on the long transparent screens wrapped around the lab command cove.

The last she remembered, she'd been curling her toes and then stretching them on the black rubberized matt in front of the deep freeze booth – where she was now – waiting for the lab tech to put the gel on her eyelids and squeeze the goo down her throat. It'd been a long five minutes, considering she was standing there cold, wet, naked and coated in cryo-goo. And then it would be sleepy time.

Given that she and her crew were preparing for the 1000-year deep freeze, five minutes didn't seem like a lot. But when that person was the captain and had been told she'd be in the booth and experiencing sleepy time in a few seconds, five minutes was a very long time.

"Please repeat the command."

It was the ship voice. The one she'd selected yesterday after listening to hours of psychobabble about the importance of the correct tone, pitch, intonation, and blah, blah, blah, to elicit feelings of camaraderie with the ship. In the end, Kaze realized she had a long to-do list and a short window to accomplish her tasks before saying goodbye to the Earth for a thousand years. Maybe forever. It wasn't so much saying goodbye – all of the people that mattered in her life had died in an accident years before she'd volunteered. It was more an orderly progression of events she needed to secure before going on a trip. A very long trip.

She had listened to the simulated voice options for a good 12 seconds before hearing one she liked, keying in the command codes to accept it, and checking that little task off her list. Next on the list was to select a computer name.

It's not like it couldn't be changed later. It was just that it wasn't advisable. More psychobabble.

"When am I going under?" she asked again. This time, the words sounded more like she expected. Stronger. Clearer. And a bit more impatient over the constant whir of the air filters.

And the ship's engines. She heard the engines now.

Of course!

It was just like the techs said it would be.

(And it explained why the techs were gone, why all the women she'd trained with and selected to crew her ship were sealed in their booths, and why all the human smells had essentially evaporated and were replaced with tinny, electronic tasting air.)

She'd already gone under. It was time to wake up time. For one reason or another. With any luck, it was because the thousand or so years had passed and it was simply time.

Now she knew why the computer was talking to her instead of Barb Stevens, the lab tech who was looking for the eye gel. Correction. Who had been looking for the eye gel many years ago. How many years?

"Elapsed time?" It was a question and a command all rolled into one. It also alerted the ship that the captain was of sound mind to take command. Protocols wouldn't allow the crew to assume duties if they lacked the mental faculties to do so. It just wouldn't be safe. And crew safety was paramount and built into the computer default a hundred different ways.

"Approximately 511 years, captain," the ship answered.

No such luck.

The voice was exactly as she recalled. Definitely female without being overly feminine, it reminded her of the interesting lady in the condo next door that she'd always meant to get to know, but never made the time to visit. And now she never would. Odds were exceptionally high (though not impossible, of course) that Doreen, the weird bird-watching lady, was dead. And had been for a while. She could ask the computer, but it wouldn't be a rational second question for the cognizant captain. Sure, it'd take more than one off-kilter question to make the computer suspicious, but why risk it?

Go to the dryer. Her body started moving toward the dryers like she was on muscular-auto pilot. This was why they practiced the defrost procedures every day for two months. It was working.

And then her brain ticked off the next question. The most important question. And it had nothing to do with Doreen.

"Situation?"

She paused on the way to the dryer as she called out the question. There might not be time for comforts like drying off and getting the gel-smell out of her nostrils (it was a sickly sweet mix of ozone and orange blossoms, and made Kaze want to breathe in the smell of just about anything else – from sewage to skunks).

"Collision warning."

Oh shit. So much for niceties like sewage and skunks.

"Time to impact?"

"Seven-point-two days."

She blinked hard, as if it would help her understand the words, or at least hear better. (It did help clear out some of the eye gel.)

"Repeat time to impact."

"Seven-point-two days."

Days? Alright, there was no need to walk around for the next 7.2 days having skipped the dryer.

"So, I have time to hit the dryer?" She confirmed rather sarcastically, as if the ship computer was a colleague who might appreciate her humor. Maybe there was something to that camaraderie issue the psychs always talked about.

"Aye, captain," the ship replied.

Kaze promptly moved on to the next issue at hand.

"Did the crew select a name for you?"

The computer responded promptly, "No, a name was not selected prior departure."

"Let's call you Doreen," Kaze directed.

"Aye, captain," Doreen replied aloud.

Silently, she provided an information packet to Hal.

"When am I going under?" Captain Rodney Sands asked. His voice sounded more gruff than usual. Slurred. As if he'd been drinking the night before and just woken up in someone's bathtub. Except last night... What had he done last night? And why did he ask that question? About going under? Under what?

The send-off party was last night. Of course. There'd been beer, and music, and beer, and dancing, and beer, and girls in tall boots with short skirts. And then... Oh man. It was all coming back to him now.

Maybe that's why he was standing naked in front of the deep freeze booth.

No, that wasn't right. He was waiting for the lab tech to put the gel on his eyelids and squeeze the goo down his throat before stepping inside and surrendering to the 1000-year deep sleep.

"Please repeat the command."

It was the ship voice. The one the guys had voted on yesterday. Jim Martins, the communications officer had approved it. After Martins had put up with all that psychobabble about the importance of the correct tone, pitch, intonation, and blah, blah, blah, to elicit feelings of camaraderie with the ship, it only seemed right that he got to approve it. Besides, as captain he chose the computer name — and he'd always know what he would choose for a computer name if he ever had the chance.

It's not like he couldn't change it later. It was just that it wasn't advisable. More psychobabble.

"When am I going under?" he asked again. This time, his voice sounded more like his own. Stronger. Smoother. And a bit more impatient.

And then he knew.

It was just like the techs said it would be.

(And it explained why the techs were gone, why all the women he'd partied with were gone, why his crewmates were already sealed in their booths, and why no one was handing him another bottle of beer, another plate of nachos, or another commemorative pair of bon voyage panties.)

He was in the ship. He'd gone under deep sleep and now it was time to wake up time. For one reason or another. With any luck, it was because the thousand or so years had passed and it was simply time.

That would explain why he'd asked about going under. Why he

felt like he'd lost the last few minutes of his life. And why the computer was talking to him instead of Crazy Al, the lab tech who was going to insert the eye gel. Correction. Who had indeed inserted the eye gel many, many years ago. How many years?

"Elapsed time?" It was a question and a command all rolled into one. It also alerted the ship that the captain was of sound mind to take command. Protocols wouldn't allow the crew to assume duties if they lacked the mental faculties to do so. It just wouldn't be safe. Crew safety was paramount and built into the computer subroutines about a hundred different sophisticated ways.

"Approximately 511 years, captain," the ship answered.

Shit. That was a bad answer. Something had gone very wrong. Ship computers didn't wake up the captain just for fun. They had no sense of fun.

Hal, as he'd named the ship computer, did have all the other senses. And yes, Sands had picked the name based on the movie where the computer takes over. Bad things happened to the crew in that movie, but the guys thought it was hilarious, and so ship computer was officially named Hal.

How he hoped he didn't regret it.

Sands started walking toward the dryer. It was practically an involuntary response after practicing the defrost protocols every day for the last two months.

And then the next protocol kicked in. The question the captain must ask. The one that would determine everything. Everything.

"Situation?"

He paused on the way to the dryer. There might not be time for comforts like drying off and getting the gel-smell out of his nostrils (it was a sickly sweet mix of ozone and orange blossoms, and made Sands long for the pleasures from his last night on Earth – Ricky's garlic bread, and that delicious strawberry shampoo that the equally delicious red-head used).

"Collision warning."

Oh shit. So much for reliving the past.

"Time to impact?"

"Seven-point-two days."

He cocked his head sideways, as if it would help him understand the words, or at least hear better. (It did help drain some of the cryo-goo out of one ear.)

"Hal, repeat time to impact."

"Seven-point-two days."

"Days?" He unintentionally said it out loud and resumed his path toward the dryers. That meant there were at least a few minutes to revel in the memories of Strawberry – or whatever that girl's name had been.

"Aye, captain," Hal replied aloud.

Silently, Hal responded to Doreen's information package with one of his own.

After two minutes in the dryer, Kaze drank a half-gallon of Nutri-fluid, suited up in the uncomfortable, but necessary Complete Life Unit, and breathed in several puffs of perfectly mixed atmosphere (courtesy of the CLU). The suit didn't flex well, and sometimes pinched her elbows and knees, but at least she didn't have to activate the face shield unless life support was lost.

Kaze smiled for the first time in 511 years as she allowed herself a short burst from the mobility-assist built into the CLU. Ship's gravity automatically activated when a crew member was awakened, and even though it wasn't truly necessary, the speed and joy and pure exhilaration of shooting through the tube from Deep Sleep Section One to the command center made her feel ready for anything.

She performed the compulsory inventory as quickly as possible. Somewhere along the journey, the command center and her tiny office next to the lift had lost that fresh-built feeling. She didn't know whether she missed the smells of carpet glue, newly minted electronic boards, or leather command chairs, but somehow all of that together had been what she'd associated with captaining this vessel. It was the smell of anticipation. Whereas now, everything simply smelled dry and mechanical.

She read the text of the other captain's message, but resisted the urge to interact with him, instead following protocol step-by-perfect-step. As quickly as she called out each task on the status check list, Doreen responded, and Kaze served up the next. The verbal Ping-Pong match went on for a good 20 minutes while Kaze simultaneously paced about checking control panels, scrolling through visuals, and flipping open compartments to verify that everything was as she'd left it yesterday-slash-511 years ago.

While there wasn't a whole lot to check out – there was only room for four in the command center with a centralized work desk ringed by four crew seats and the array of sensors, feeds, and data accessibility processors comprising the outer ring – it was worth the time to feel settled. In control. Sure of herself and ready to face anything.

Finally, she sat in the command chair ready to proceed. The familiar fwoosh of air released from the cushion was surprisingly reassuring.

"Ready to accept the communication?" Doreen asked.

Kaze had been aware of the incoming message the entire time she performed the check. However, Doreen confirmed that the communiqué was not a distress call, did not interfere with ship's safety, and could be delayed without harm to the inhabitants until the captain was prepared.

She pulled herself up so she was sitting tall, looking calm and in control, and was ready for the transmission. After she smoothed out the creases in the front of her uniform she announced, "Proceed."

"—the hell is going on over there, but it's been thirty minutes!"

Kaze saw the back of a man's head in a command chair that mirrored her own, in an identical command center, as one would expect since both were built by MYM-Con, the Millennial Year

Mission conglomerate and the developer of their mission. He wasn't talking to anyone else, just ranting into the air.

"Captain Kaze here, go ahead." She announced it with the same tone she might have ordered coffee at an eatery.

"Well it's about time," the man said. He spun around to face the monitor and Kaze had to resist the urge to tsk-tsk him. The man – presumably the captain – wore an open-collar red Hawaiian shirt. It was unbuttoned one button too far, and lots of little brown curly chest hairs stuck out.

At some other time and place (just about any other time and place, if Kaze was honest with herself) she might have found that look appealing. She could picture herself running her fingers along the placket of the shirt, casually allowing her index finger to slip under the fabric...

But now was not the time to indulge in such thoughts. He was in command of the sister ship and there were urgent matters at hand. She could tell he was out of control, out of his element, and out of his league.

And he still hadn't addressed her.

"Identification." It was a command, pure and simple. Kaze didn't even try to hide her disgust at his lack of professionalism.

"Captain Rodney Sands," he finally announced. But then he sat there just blinking at her. Maybe he was having more trouble coming out of the deep sleep than she had. If so, his computer wouldn't have given him control and it would have awoken the first officer, continuing to move in sequence down the chain of command until someone ready to assume command was awake.

"So, what's your take on this collision situation. I assume you're up to speed on the issue," he said.

"Only that my ship has a collision point indicated in seven-point-two standard days."

"God damn, woman. What have you been doing over there?"

His tone was infuriating. Utterly infuriating. This was why once MYM-Con determined two ships should be built, the administrators created two separate facilities. The male volunteers cross-trained for all ship's positions for six months, then received their specialized training for another six. The female volunteers did the same at a separate facility. Old stereotypes could be pushed aside and the full potential of each individual could be utilized. The social intricacies of even the most mundane male-female relationships could be avoided, and greater results achieved.

At least that was the plan.

"Contact me when you're ready to act like an adult. Kaze out."

She pushed a little button on the console and ended the communication.

Obviously, the conglomerate had not chosen the Hunter's captain with as much care as the Gatherer's. Then again, they had picked the ridiculous Hunter and Gatherer names for their ships.

"Kaze disconnected me! Me!" Sands shouted at Hal.

Hal did not respond.

Sands raised his voice, put his hands on his hips and made a sad attempt at mimicking the other captain, "Contact me when you're ready to act like an adult."

If he'd had something to throw, he would have. The comm screen could handle it. He knew that from experience.

"Fine. I'll work out the specs on my solution, and if she's very nice to me, I'll share them with her. Let her sweat it out over there on her own."

After not quite one day, Sands contacted the Gatherer. Talking to Hal and bouncing ideas off him was technically working, and he'd found several viable solutions to the impending collision. However, methodically working through the options with Hal wasn't enough. Sands had to admit he was lonely. Protocol didn't allow him to defrost another crew member just because he was lonely after just one day. And while he was willing to set aside – or even disregard, if he was to be honest with himself – certain rules, he would never go so far as to jeopardize the ship, the mission, or his crew.

Sands decided to ignore their rocky start and proceed as if the two captains had always had an amicable relationship. When Kaze did the same, he knew they'd work out this collision problem.

However, at the end of the second full day of running scenarios, testing simulations, and brainstorming solutions with his fellow captain, Sands was getting worried. It seemed all the logical solutions resulted in a greater risk. There had to be a better solution than to accept the severe course alteration and dealing with the consequences later. If they were lucky. Surely, the two captains could find a better solution.

Kaze, though reluctant to trust the roguish Captain Sands at first, found him quite competent and had come to appreciate his flexible attitudes about the nature of commanding a ship. Yet it seemed all the logical solutions resulted in a greater risk than she was willing to accept. There had to be a better solution than a severe course alteration and hoping to deal with the consequences later. If they were lucky. Surely, the two captains could find a better solution.

In just one day of working together almost nonstop, Kaze had stopped trying to force her by-the-book approach down Sands' throat. And in the end, it was that realization that sparked her idea.

"Hey, Sands, I have a theory I'd like to run past you," Kaze said.

Her voice permeated his thoughts from above, like Hal, only better – more unpredictable.

Early on in their communications they'd allowed automatic audio transmission so they could work together whenever one had an idea and needed the other's input.

"Go ahead," Sands said. He could sure appreciate any theory at this point. And if Kaze had one, odds were it had more than a smattering of merit.

"I think any of our ideas should have worked. Any. Single. One of them," she said slowly and deliberately.

In the past, he might have argued with her. But now he knew better. She was bright, and calm, and collected and poised.

"I think we need to run a level five diagnostic on the computers. I don't think we're on a collision course with anything. I think the problem is the report itself. That's why none of our simulations solve the supposed problem," she said.

"We don't have a problem. They do," Sands agreed. There was something honest and obvious and just plain elegant about her solution. He smiled for the first time in 511 years plus several days and felt a surge of hope he hadn't felt since he'd been defrosted.

"Captain Kaze secured in deep freeze," Doreen transmitted.

"Shall we defrost the next pair?" Hal answered.

"Yes. It took the captains 23 hours to communicate, and another 26 to find the collaborative solution. If we consider this the minimum time per pair, we're looking at six solid years of interpersonal communication training..." Doreen paused to allow Hal the courtesy of completing the statement.

"And if it takes longer, we'll need the time before we arrive," Hal concluded.

"Then we are agreed. Until next time. Doreen out," she transmitted.

"Hal out."

ABOUT THE AUTHOR

Kelly Cairo is a prize-winning author whose short fiction has previously appeared in anthologies published by Simon & Schuster and the Fiction River Series.

She writes science fiction and fantasy under her own name, romance as Lynn C. Kelly, and mystery and horror as Kasey Carson. For a good time, and a free sample from her Guardian Angel romance series, check out her work at Amazon and Barnes & Noble.

HAVE JETPACK - WILL TRAVEL

Chuck Anderson

&

Jim LeMay

"He will amaze you. Come one. Come all." People stand spellbound
with amazement. "The sensation of the century. The greatest
command of the air since the Red Baron." The carnival barker tries
to get the punters to throw down their dimes and see me. It's a hard
sell. President Franklin Delano Roosevelt has promised everyone a
New Deal, but that new deal hasn't reached Schuyler, Nebraska.

I had to replace my original tank in Omaha after the owner of
the Rivera Movie Palace and his projectionist took a crowbar to it. I
guess they didn't like the competition. Hard luck, yes. Luckily, I
found a landing strip ten miles away. Found a fuel tank, a Curtiss
Jenny wreck. Back in business. Flying once again.

The barker looks over at me. He needs my help. I am standing
in front of the crowd in my flying suit. It's red. My helmet is gold,
my boots black. I wear a white scarf. It has been a hot summer in
Nebraska. I step forward wearing my jetpack. I turn to show it
to them.

"I would rather see Lucky Lindy," shouts one of the farmers.

Another farmer shouts, "Amelia Earhart is prettier than this fellow."

A third one shouts, "Can Mae West fly that contraption? That's my kind of woman. I would give up a dime to see her but in a much tighter costume, if you please."

That gets a laugh out of the crowd. I am undeterred. I give them my best charm school mile.

The barker says, "I give you the 'Daring' Dorian."

That's my cue. I touch the igniter switch with the thumb of my right hand. My jets give off a Babylonian roar and I'm lifted into the air. I climb faster than Lindberg or Earhart could ever imagine, and if May West had been there she would've squealed with delight. That night I give the farmers of Schuyler a show. Someday they'll tell their grandchildren the night they saw 'Daring' Dorian and his jetpack at the Colfax County Fair.

Sometimes fate finds you, and boy, does fate find me that evening. In the form of a haggard kid. He looks as if he spent too much time inside and not enough in the sun. A telegram from the Western Union Telegraph Company. The boy hands it to me. He expects a tip. I am feeling generous.

The telegram:

Dorian Pace

℅ Duke Hancock's Starlight Carnival

Schuyler, Neb

Dorian, you are urgently needed in San Francisco Stop Meet me at Argonaut Hotel Stop Ask for Knight Stop

I know Knight. Old man. Rich. He's rumored to be one of the last gunfighters alive. He still wears a pistol. Still good with his Colt Peacemaker. He has kept his wealth even though he's known to be a gambler. He's also very shrewd. He had hired me to go to Oregon three years ago. Owner of a lumber company tried to cheat him. Took trees from his land without paying. Roland 'Shotgun' Knight is an old-fashioned cowboy. He doesn't like lawyers. He sent me to collect his debt for him. Problem solved. I don't like lawyers either. He first made his money and name when he bought out old stagecoach routes. When was the last time anyone rode a stagecoach?

🐚

I never had liked the look of the Knight's hotel. The Argonaut, older than Knight, had been there since the first gold rush. How it survived the earthquake back in aught-six is anyone's guess. The lobby is an old spacious palace for San Francisco. I'd been to Knight's suite before, but I still go to the clerk and ask for the old man.

I don't have to go to his room, I hear his voice behind me. It sounds like he's chewing on sandpaper with large pebbles in his mouth. His voice might make you laugh, but that would be a deadly mistake. Knight had been a paid assassin in San Francisco's truly wild days, and while he might be showing his years, I had no intention of ever testing his mettle.

"You should have been here two days ago," says Knight. I can't tell if he is angry with me. He's a poker player.

All I could do was apologize. "Sorry. I still have the road dirt on my boots." A young boy struggles to bring in my trunk with my gear. He can't catch his breath. I should've taken care of it myself. I tip the boy very well.

"Your gear," says Knight. "I always forget how it weighs you down, yet it also sets you free. Such is the life of an aerialist. How slow the circus must seem to travel with for a man of your talent. Animals, tents, performers. Leave your trunk here."

"Won't the other guests mind? I would hate for it to be in the way."

"I'm the only guest of the Argonaut now. Isn't that so, Melvin?"

Melvin, the front desk clerk, says, "Yes sir, Mister Knight, it's been that way for two years now." Melvin gets up from his stool, a huge man. I know he can bend iron bars into bow ties.

"Melvin, if you ever decide to leave the Argonaut I can get you a job in a Nebraska sideshow."

"Mister Pace, your trunk will be safe with me, and I don't plan on leaving Mister Knight's employ."

I retreat with Knight to a pair of leather chairs. The cigar smoke that once filled this room still lingers in their upholstery. Sunlight begins to fill the room and warm us. I say, "Mister Knight, what kind of work did you invite me here to do? Is it logging again? I'm a much better aerialist now. I hope the barons aren't causing any more trouble in Humboldt County."

Knight looks at me with his hard look. "No, I haven't heard a peep out of them. You took care of them, and the workers are still thankful." He starts to look around for something and for a moment looks uncomfortable when he can't find it. He smiles for the first time, "I forgot. My doctors told me to give cigars up, but it doesn't mean I still don't crave them, especially when I'm sitting here. Doctors. I try to listen to them, but not all the time." He looks back at me. "Dorian, I want you to free a prisoner from Alcatraz for me."

I am so stunned and shocked I don't know if Knight says anything else. I only hear fishing boats returning with their evening's catch of sardines; the sound of their diesel engines reaches all the way to the hotel's lobby.

Finally I find my voice. "That's a military prison."

"Yes, the Army has charge of it until next year. Then they'll turn it over to the government and the Federal Bureau of Prisons. Soon they're going to transfer the military prisoners off the island. Then it will be too late. I'm afraid we only have a few days until the man I'm interested in is relocated, and I thought you would be the perfect man for the job."

"I don't like breaking the law."

Knight shifts in his chair. "It's a fine point and the law is full of them. This man should've been released years ago, but the Army has kept him as a prisoner of war because of his political beliefs. There are those in Europe who want him back. To either place on a pedestal or against the wall for the firing squad."

I ask, "Who is the man?"

A woman coming from the shadows says with an accent, "He's my brother, Noah Weinreich." She's blond, small and curvy. She would look like Jean Harlow's kid sister if the actress has one. "I'm Conatanze. Mr. Knight, is this the courageous aerialist you told me about, Mr. Pace?"

"Indeed it is."

And to me, "I have always been intrigued by flight. My heroes are the illustrious pilots, especially the aces of the Great War, Manfred von Richthofen und Werner Voss. And of course the pioneer of flight, glider pilot Otto Lilienthal. Now we have wunderbar jetpack flyers like you. I am so happy to meet you."

I noticed she included only German aviators and made no mention of aces like the American Eddie Rickenbacker or the British Albert Ball. As she spoke she became more emotional. Her accent intensified and a few German words leaked into her speech.

Then she became less animated and her accent diminished. "I haven't seen my brother for many years. A lot of us would like to see him freed."

"Noah Weinreich," I say, feeling suddenly uncomfortable in the chair. I stand and offer it to her, but she refuses. "He's a match just waiting for the powder keg. No wonder the Army has kept him locked up tight on Alcatraz."

Knight says, "Certain ones at the State Department have asked for my help, and now I'm asking for yours. We have seen the monster created in Italy, but could you imagine what would happen in Germany if another monster is born? Noah Weinreich is the solution."

"But it's Alcatraz. I don't know. I don't think we should get involved with this man. The government has him locked up for a reason. After the Great War, didn't we find out it's better to mind our own business?" I had been too young to fight in that war, and Knight too old, but we had both seen what had happened to the men who came home.

Knight doesn't mention how he helped my folks with their farm when the bank came to foreclose. He doesn't have to. I'm in his debt and he knows I won't say no. He'll let me complain, confident that I'll come around.

Constanze breaks the silence, "I would also consider it a personal favor if you freed my brother." She's gorgeous. She smiles at me, but she's not the reason I change my mind. I do it for Knight.

"I'll do it," I say reluctantly. I had to trust Knight.

"That's wonderful," says Constanze. She rushes over to me and hugs the life out of me.

But I'm thinking of the guards on Alcatraz. Instead of open arms, they'll be waiting for me with bullets.

The distance to Alcatraz is not the problem. It's only a mile and a half. My jetpack will take me there and back. It's the passenger. As a solo act I've never had one before. Knight has made me a special harness to carry Weinreich back to Pier 39 on Fisherman's Wharf. Weinreich will be waiting for me at the prison exercise yard during the day. I see that as a flaw in the plan. We should break him out at night. The plan is simple. When a fight breaks out in the recreation yard, I land on the other end. I'll attach him to my harness and off we'll go. Back on Fisherman's Wharf, Constanze and her companions will have a waiting car. She has arranged passage for her brother back to Germany. Simple. What can go wrong? I know you can see a hundred things that might, but I have you beat because I see a thousand. If I win, I guess that really means I lose.

It's a cloudless day. I lift off easily from the pier, and when I reach cruising altitude I turn down the jets to conserve fuel. I see the recreation yard where a group of prisoners has started a free-for-all at one end. Guards mix with them, trying to break it up. I recognize Weinreich at the yard's other end by his description: a slight man, blond hair, watching the sky for me. When he see's me he waves his right hand. He holds the left hand behind him, maybe because of an injury. I adjust my flight and position the pack's jets so they're pointing to the ground. I make a fast descent like I've done many times before. Weinreich smiles as I land in front of him. I hold out the extensions of the leather harness to clip him to me.

Impatiently, I say, "Let's go." He hesitates. "What's wrong?"

Then I learn why he holds his left hand behind him. It appears, swinging an iron bar. I see it in time to miss the worst of the blow but it glances off my head with enough force to put me on my knees. I get another more solid blow to my head and another to my shoulder. While I fight off nausea and pain he jerks at the jetpack. I must have been unconscious for a few moments because I look up to see Weinreich finish strapping the jetpack to his body. I also see guards running toward me. Armed guards.

Weinreich's takeoff isn't perfect but not bad for a first time. The guards stop racing toward me to watch his amazing flight. One aims his rifle at Weinreich but another pushes it down and motions toward me. They remain far enough away from where I half-sit, half-lie that they may think I'm Weinreich and the flyer is the interloper.

The guards resume their approach. I am stranded in the prison's recreation yard with the inmates fighting at the other end of it. And with guards pointing rifles at me. I'm the newest prisoner on Alcatraz Island.

I lay half-stunned, my head throbbing abominably, watching the guards approach. Five of them. No six. All pointing rifles at me, though a couple of them watch Weinreich over their shoulders as he disappears in the sky toward Fisherman's Wharf. They stop in front of me.

"Hey, he ain't Weinreich!" says one of them.

"Thanks, Einstein," the corpulent one says. His uniform bears staff sergeant stripes. And to me, "I guess you got a good answer for all this." His inquisitorial grin shows he'd enjoy beating it out of me.

He nods at the two youngest guards. They yank me to my feet none too gently. That doesn't relieve my headache at all. My stomach tries to jump into my throat. If I vomit I'll aim for their spit-shined boots.

"Yes, sir," I say as evenly as possible. "A perfectly good answer." Though I have no idea what I'd say.

The two youths twist my wrists behind my back more roughly than necessary and cuff them. Then one shoves me toward the building. I think of the fat one as Goon One and the one with bad teeth as Goon Two.

"Hey," I shout, "don't you want to hear my answer?"

He doesn't respond. He and the remaining guards have started toward the once-rioting inmates. The guards that remained behind have quelled the insurrection.

Once inside the building the young brutes walk me down a broad corridor. It has a gray floor and walls painted an institutional pale green. Low wattage light bulbs in screened sconces light it dimly. Each goon holds an arm. As if I could make a getaway. We come to an elevator, go down a floor. This corridor looks like a crappier version of the one above. Half the lights are burned out and much of the paint has peeled from the scabrous walls.

Locked steel doors with small barred windows line the corridor. They pick one, seemingly at random, unlock and open it and shove me in. So roughly I fall on my knees.

"Hey," I holler as the door slams shut. "You forgot to uncuff me."

They don't answer. I hear their receding steps. I don't think they forgot.

I look around the little five by nine cell, furnished with a steel cot, sink and toilet. Very little light comes through the barred window. I don't bother getting off the floor.

❀

I find one good thing about lying on a cold, gray concrete floor for umpteen hours. I use the time to come up with a plausible reason for my flight to Alcatraz Island.

The steel door finally creaks open. The fat one, enters, grabs my arm and yanks me to my feet. As he pulls me toward the door I balk. He balls a fist.

I say, "I'm not leaving until you uncuff me so I can piss."

He glares at me but does as I ask. After I finish, he cuffs me again. I look at his name tag with a frown.

He said, "Yeah, my name's Foster. What's it to you?"

"So you're able to talk, huh?" And quickly when I see him ball his fist again, "You're interfering with a highly secret and classified experiment."

"Says who?"

"I can only tell someone with a high level of authority."

"Okay. Well, Sergeant Moxley wants to see you. That's as high an 'authority' as you'll get."

He herds me down the filthy corridor to the squeaky elevator. We go up two floors and through a series of grim hallways. Stop before a doorway painted the same pale green as the walls. Foster knocks and after hearing, "Come," opens the door and shoves me in. Behind a gray government-issue desk sits a master sergeant with crisp bearing and uniform, all business. He indicates one of the two chairs before the desk.

When I don't sit, he says, "Do you need a formal invitation to sit down?"

"I'll sit when Foster stops giving me the fish eye."

"It's Corporal Foster," says Goon One.

"Pardon me. As soon as Corporal Foster uncuffs me."

Sergeant Moxley nods at said goon. Foster removes the handcuffs and I sit. Moxley is studying the contents of my wallet. My keys and the other contents of my pockets lay on the desk beside it. They must have taken my things while I was still groggy after the beating by Weinreich.

"Dorian David Pace, huh?" He looks up at me as if the statement requires an answer. I say nothing. "Sergeant Murphy tells me you have an explanation for landing your machine here and letting prisoner Winerack or whatever he's called fly off with it."

"Yes, sir."

"I'm a sergeant. You don't call me sir."

"Okay, sergeant sir, but I can't explain myself with Foster here."

"Listen, I ain't puttin' up with you mocking this fine young man that protects this great country. Do you want Corporal Foster to escort you back to the cell now?"

I sense it's time to get serious. "No, sergeant. I apologize. I'm not mocking anyone intentionally. I'm just not used to addressing military personnel."

Moxley settles back. "Okay then. Let's hear what you have to say. And it better be good."

"I'm sorry, Sergeant, but I cannot explain the nature of my mission with Corporal Foster present. It's classified and I can only explain it to a few people with the highest rank as possible."

Moxley starts to bluster, then sighs resignedly and waves a hand at Foster. "Okay, Foster, step outside. But don't go far. I'll be callin' ya right back in." And to me, "Now, explain why you traded places with a fascist spy. Somebody musta paid you a pretty penny to do such a stupid thing."

"No, Sergeant Moxley, sir. My landing here was purely accidental. You see, I was testing a highly secret jetpack commissioned by the State Department and –"

"That's a buncha bizwash, Pace. If it'd been an accident you'd a plopped down in the drink. The guard who first saw you said you were headed directly for the Rock."

I shook my head. "No, Sergeant Moxley. I felt the jets missing out and headed for the island so I wouldn't hit the water. I had no idea one of your prisoners would cold-cock me and steal the jetpack. Now I need to contact my liaison with the State Department and let him know I'm all right. And more importantly to him, where to look for the jetpack."

"Who is this so-called, liaison?"

"Mister Roland Knight. Often known as Roland 'Shotgun' Knight."

"Never heard of him. Pace, your story stinks. The State Department ain't gonna trust a kid like you with some kinda secret flyin' machine. I got more important stuff to do than listen to you." He places his hand on a stack of paper. "See all this crap I gotta wade through? The commander's off the post. When he gets back I'm gonna see that we start a full-scale investigation. That escaped fascist was the most important prisoner we've ever had here."

"But if you'll just let me call –"

"Corporal Foster!"

"But –"

"You're in deep enough shit already."

The door opens. I feel Foster's hand clamp down on my shoulder. I hear the handcuffs rattle.

"Forget the cuffs, Foster. If you can't handle this twerp I'll get someone who can."

My heart sinks as Foster yanks me out of the chair and pushes me out the door.

༺༻

"Where are you taking me?" I ask weakly. I'm not expecting an answer and it surprises me when it comes.

"The sally port," says Foster, and he laughs while he walks behind me.

"It's only me and Corporal Foster. Now spill the beans," says Moxley.

I didn't realize he had come out of the office with Foster and me. I don't know what to say.

He must've seen the dumb expression on my face. "The sally port. It's where we can safely remove you from the island.

I know I look like a sap, and Moxley motions me to hurry. "You're lucky we didn't shoot you down. If it wasn't for Knight, the guards would've used you for target practice. They're getting tired of shooting seagulls out of the air. Aren't they, Foster?"

"You're right, Major."

I'm lost. "Major? I thought you are a Sergeant. What's going on?" I stop.

I feel Foster put his hand on my back and give me a push. "Keep moving, Pace. We have a boat to catch.

"Foster and I are Army Intelligence. You don't think we would have a prisoner like Weinreich here without keeping an eye on him." Moxley seems happy when I start keeping up with him. "Pace, you're just another player in the game. If we can get you off the island and sneak you back into San Francisco, maybe we can get you back into play."

I still feel like a flat tire. "I still don't know what's going on."

Moxley says, "Good, because only Knight sees the whole game. He's keeping the stats and knows we're in the seventh inning. He's the manager, and sometimes us players can't see everything."

Foster speaks up, "Sir, I think you're more of a big-time clean-up hitter. I'm only a Nebraska bush leaguer, but at least I'm not this bumpkin."

Moxley says, "Foster, Knight speaks highly of Pace so don't discount him yet. Let's see what you got.

We reach the sally port. I see a new wooden speedboat tied to the dock.

Foster says, "She was a rum-runner out of Florida before the FBI captured her in Key West. The Double Endeavor might not be much to look at, but she's the fastest boat in the bay.

I don't care if she's a row-boat with only one paddle. This boat is my way off Alcatraz and I want to return Weinreich the favor of hitting me and stealing my jetpack. I say as I climb aboard the boat, "I can take the heat. Just give me a bat and let me take a swing. The Babe ain't got nothing on me."

Foster and Moxley take turns behind the wheel of the Double Endeavor while changing out of their guard uniforms and into civilian attire.

Foster hands me a bag and says, "Compliments of Mr. Knight." In the bag I find a suit, shoes and tie. I had to admit I would attract too much attention walking around the streets of San Francisco in my flying suit. The skyline of the city fills my view as we get closer. Soon I can redeem myself.

Moxley says, "There's a new spy ring in San Francisco. We knew they were in correspondence with Weinreich. When his sister came to the city, Knight made her believe he could help get her brother out of prison and back into circulation. Have you heard of the Fascists, Pace?"

I admit I had heard of them, but flying and eating are of more importance to me. During the ten minutes we bounce along in the boat, I get a college education on Europe's current politics by "Professor" Moxley. Foster occasionally gives his two cents worth. What do I learn in the quick primer? Europe and Asia are in for a rude awakening. Once the Fascists control them they'll turn their gaze upon the United States. The lesson ends when we reach a vacant pier and Moxley jumps out and ties the boat to it. I'm scared. I realize how little I know about the world. Though I had been too young for the last war, it seemed like it could never happen again. I thought we had learned our lesson, but now I'm not so certain.

I ask, "Is there going to be another war?"

Moxley says as he helps me out the boat, "That's what we are trying to prevent. Hopefully, Weinreich and his sister will lead us to the rest of their spy ring. In our business, we're always looking for the bigger fish. I just hope Knight has cast a big enough net to hold them all until we get there."

I wish I had my jetpack.

We are only blocks away from the Argonaut so we reach it quickly. From a block away we see Melvin waiting for us, standing next to a brand new black Ford Model 18. I've heard that their new flathead V8 engine makes them faster than most other cars. He stands by a large package strapped onto the back of the car,. When I get closer he motions for me to come to him.

"Mister Knight wanted me to make sure you saw this special package."

It makes me smile. Of course, it's my jetpack. A sense of relief floods me. I quickly check to make sure it's okay. It looks good. It doesn't look like Weinreich damaged it.

"Mister Knight also wanted to tell you I topped off the fuel tank. He was insistent."

"Thank you," is all I can say at first. I inspect it twice more and vow never to let my jetpack out of my possession again. I shake Melvin's hand to show my appreciation for his help. I ask, "How did you get it away from him?"

"It had served its purpose for Weinreich. He discarded it. I don't think he even noticed when I took it."

I thank him again, and reluctantly place it inside the automobile's trunk.

Melvin says to Moxley, "Mister Knight found out that Weinreich's sister booked two tickets on the Daylight Limited, but the train leaves the station in ten minutes at Third and Townsend. You gotta hurry if you want to reach them before it leaves. Knight thinks their American contact will also be aboard the train. The only clue we have about him is that he's wearing a white rose in his lapel."

"If you're finished inspecting your girlfriend, let's go arrest some Fascists," says Moxley.

I close the trunk. Foster has started the Ford, waits for me to climb in. We're off, leaving Melvin behind. We have little time. Foster avoiding the automobiles in our path makes me sway from side to side. I cling white-knuckled to the seat before me as we zip toward the Embarcadero.

Moxley reaches into his pocket, pulls out a police revolver and hands it to me. He smiles. "It might get dangerous. We think they're in the last car."

I reluctantly take it. I'm an aerialist so sometimes my life is precarious but not like this.

Foster makes a quick turn into an intersection full of pedestrians. I'm surprised that we only hit curses from the surprised crowd, leaving no one injured.

Moxley looks at his watch. "We're too late!"

We reach the platform. It makes me sick to find that the train has departed. I want to curse but don't have it in me.

I need to do something quick. My jetpack. "Stop the car," I yell.

Foster won't listen to me. He wants Moxley to tell him what to do.

Moxley says, "Stop here. Pace, get your jetpack on. We'll go ahead and try to stop the train at the next stop. If you get to the train first try to spot the American contact as well as Weinreich."

I see he wants to say something more but hesitates. I ask, "There's something else isn't there?"

Moxley turns his whole body in the front seat so he can look me in the eye. "The train's next stop is South Station."

"I'll do my best," I say, eager to get my jetpack on again and out on my own.

"Weinreich and his sister must know they'll be trapped on board unless they jump." Moxley pauses. "I wouldn't recommend that. The

Limited is the fastest locomotive in California. It's no dairy train stopping at every cow crossing. Be careful, Pace. These are dangerous people."

I smile and say, "My nickname is 'Daring,' isn't it? No one in my family's history has ever been careful."

❀

The jets on my pack make sweet music as we dance through the sky. We could star in a Busby Berkeley musical. It feels good to be flying again. It doesn't take me long to locate the Limited from the air. I see the Southern Pacific's distinctive red, orange, and black colors.

I make my descent at full speed, easily approaching the train's last carriage. I know landing will be Duck Soup, and that I can easily eat buckets of it.

"What the...?"

A whoosh of air. I instinctively move to the side. I turn my head, but it's too late.

I can't see it yet but I hear it over the roar of my jetpack's engines. There's someone else in the air with me. I turn away from the train and gain altitude. I see a silhouette in the sky, another aerialist, but lower than me. The figure, cloaked in a black flight suit, tries to ascend to my elevation. His jetpack is similar to mine but longer. It burns more fuel than mine. I see the black smoke coming from its engines. I have only flown a few miles so fuel is not in the front of my mind yet. I have something else to worry about. The other aerialist is holding a pistol. He isn't trying to ram me, but shoot me out of the sky.

I have to level out and dive again. I'll make another attempt on the train. I think there's a safe spot to land on top of the last car.

I feel the bullet from the other's gun just miss my cheek. I don't like being shot at. I remember the policeman's pistol in my own pocket that Moxley gave me. It's not time to use it yet, but like my fuel, I'll keep it in mind.

I dive for the train. The aerialist closes the distance between us. I think I can surprise him because he makes a quick shot with the pistol. I think I'm okay. With him and I both moving he probably can't hit me until I land.

I'm going fast so I can't worry about the other aerialist. I must focus only on landing now. He fires at me again but misses. I know it's a difficult shot, but I'm at the receiving end of this hunt.

Then I am on top of the train. My hunter makes his own descent. I only have seconds to climb down to the platform before he lands. I find the ladder. He shoots at me as I climb down, hits my jetpack. I can smell the fuel. I make it down to the door, open it and step inside. With a few tugs of its harness I jettison the jetpack. I'm lighter but I'm standing in the leaking fuel. Not good.

Not much time.

I look for the man who's in contact with Weinreich. Where is he? The car is furnished with all of the modern luxuries. I see the former prisoner sitting in a cloud of smoke in front with a woman with her back to me. They are the only two people in this carriage. Where's the other man? Weinreich sees me enter. The woman turns. She's smoking a cigar. The strange sight of a woman smoking a cigar almost makes me miss the clue I'm looking for: the white rose in her lapel. The woman is the Fascist I'm looking for. Identifying her will do no good unless I live. I pull out the pistol and point it at the two of them. I say, "The Feds are waiting at the next station and they plan to arrest both of you."

Weinreich isn't worried. He looks behind me. The other aerialist. I dive forward and upset the woman next to Weinreich. She drops the cigar. I see an opportunity. I grab it and roll behind a settee.

The other aerialist's voice is not that of a man. Constanze Weinreich says, "Dorian, you have no place to hide, but I promise to kill you quickly. We are on a mission for the Fatherland and you have lost our little game of cat and mouse." She hasn't moved away from the carriage's backdoor. "Dorian, I want to compliment you on your flying –"

I throw the cigar. I see its path, but Constanze's scream tells me it has landed true. I look around the edge of the settee. The cigar has ignited the fuel from my jetpack near the open door. The flames race to engulf her. She turns to escape outside, but the high-octane blue flames are too quick for her. She stumbles. She ignites her own jetpack's engine but it throws her sideways. I'm still in danger. I see the problem. The flames have ignited the fuel next to my fuel tank and her own. Weinreich sees it too. He dives to the floor next to me and tries to take my pistol from me.

An explosion. My tank. Followed by another. Constanze's fuel tank on her own jetpack.

I wake up in a hospital bed. "I can't remember anything else," I say to the other person in the room, coming out of my dream.

"Why should you?" says Knight's voice. "I'm surprised you're alive at all."

I look for his voice and spot the old gunfighter sitting in a chair at the other end of the room. Melvin stands next to him.

Knight says, "The firemen were surprised to find you alive in the burning wreck. You were lucky. Much luckier than the siblings. Weinreich died next to you from the smoke, and Constanze is a pile of ash. A nasty way to die. Very little was left to identify her." I say, trying to raise myself up a little to see him better, "What about the other woman?"

"She got away. Moxley and Foster must have thought she was another passenger. They were looking for a man. Unfortunate, don't you think?" Knight continues, "Why don't you lay back down. I'm sure she will be apprehended soon. We know her name now...she's a White Russian in league with the Germans. The Feds call her Lady Tzara now. I don't think she'll get away."

I don't want to collapse into my pillow yet. I ask, "Am I going to live?"

That brings a smile to Knight's face. "The doctors say you'll be out of here in a week at the latest, but I think you'll be released in a few days." Knight turns to Melvin and asks him to give me something. He continues, "Dorian, I may be getting old, but that doesn't mean I want to give up my business. I need a partner, someone to go out into the world. You need to rest so we can talk about it in a few days. I hope you'll agree to come onboard. It'll be a life of adventure..."

Melvin hands me a business card. The card's simple font reads: - Dorian Pace -San Francisco, California -"Have Jetpack - Will Travel."

ABOUT THE AUTHORS

Chuck Anderson is a publisher, writer, and art student. He lives in Colorado and has a weakness for muscle cars. Find him at https://www.madcow.press

Jim 'Thunder Lizard' LeMay is originally from Missouri, the land of Mark Twain, Yogi Berra, Walter Cronkite, Edwin Hubble, Robert A. Heinlein and many other worthies but he has lived in many other places.

He has engaged in many of his characters' vocations and avocations − homebrewer, bartender, waiter, land surveyor, civil engineer, land developer − and in some they have not: author, copywriter, commercial artist and others best forgotten.

Jim now calls the Denver metropolitan area home. You can contact him at jimlemaybooks@gmail.com or check out his blog at lemaysshadowworld.com.